ADAM GANN, OUTLAW

and Adam Gann had accidentally the friend of the circuit judge and then himself sentenced to Yuma prison. On ay to Yuma, Apaches attacked and escaped, joining a wagon train heading Arizona territory. Trouble has followed owever, and outlaws attack the wagon Gann can run no further. He must and fight, for himself, for his new s, and for one person in particular – a young woman named Sharon Mc od.

ADAM GANN, OUTLAW

by

Ray Hogan

The Golden West Large Print Books
Long Preston, North Yorkshire,
BD23 4ND, England.

British Library Cataloguing in Publication Data.

Hogan, Ray
  Adam Gann, outlaw.

  A catalogue record of this book is
  available from the British Library

  ISBN   978-1-84262-906-2 pbk

First published 1978

Copyright © 1978 by Ray Hogan

Cover illustration © Gordon Crabb by arrangement with
Alison Eldred

The moral right of the author has been asserted

Published in Large Print 2012 by arrangement with
Golden West Literary Agency

The Golden West Large Print is an imprint of Library Magna
Books Ltd.

Printed and bound in Great Britain by
T.J. (International) Ltd., Cornwall, PL28 8RW

Chapter 1

'Want you getting this straight – first off,' Frank Slawson said in his hard, grim way. 'You make one wrong move and I'll blow your head off!'

Adam Gann stared woodenly at the lawman, a deputy U.S. marshal sent to escort him to Yuma Prison.

'I won't give you no trouble.'

'You sure as hell better not!' Slawson snapped, and suddenly drawing his pistol, clubbed Gann across the temple and sent him stumbling up against the wall.

Dave Hayden, sheriff at Lordsburg, sitting at his desk in his small, heat-filled office, rose angrily.

'Now, why'd you go an' do that?' he demanded, frowning. 'Weren't no cause–'

'Just want him remembering what I said,' Slawson replied coldly, holstering his weapon.

Hayden had moved out from behind his desk to the center of the room. It was hot for May, and sweat glistened on the faces of the three men. Outside, in Lordsburg's main street, it was business as usual with no one paying any attention to what was taking place inside the jail.

'He told you he'd go along peaceable, didn't he?' Hayden continued, halting in front of Gann, who was now staring at Slawson with steady, narrowed eyes. The raised sight on the marshal's pistol had cut a small gash in the skin above his ear, and a dark welt was rapidly forming.

'Man would be a fool to take an outlaw's word on anything,' Slawson said indifferently.

'Maybe, but Gann ain't your run-of-the-mill outlaw,' Hayden, a lean elderly man with a quick, nervous way about him, insisted.

'Busted out of the jail at Paradise, didn't he?'

'Yeh, but he had a reason.'

Slawson's patient smile held no humor. About thirty, he was short, thick-shouldered, sharp-faced, balding, and had dark, agate-like eyes. His mouth, partly shadowed by a full mustache, was scarcely more than a straight, grim line. One glance at the lawman's unforgiving features provided an index to the man's savage nature.

'No, I reckon that ain't so,' he drawled, brushing at the sweat collected on his forehead. 'Boils down to this – he was a killer, convicted, and waiting to be taken to Yuma. He broke jail–'

'And come straight here,' Hayden cut in. 'Had to do it that way because the sheriff up there at Paradise couldn't be bothered to bring him down here so's he could take care of some personal business.'

Slawson shrugged, stared out the dust-filmed window. 'I ain't interested in why's–'

'Business that concerned his sister – sending his belongings to her over in Illinois – along with the money he was getting from selling his horse and gear.'

'The law ain't interested either in–'

'It's about time the law used a little good sense,' Hayden declared, not at all intimidated by the federal lawman. 'Goes for you, too!'

Slawson came about, settled his cold glance on the older man. 'Meaning?'

Gann, stunned briefly by the unexpected blow dealt him by the marshal but now fully recovered, listened quietly to the exchange between the two lawmen. He appreciated Hayden's coming to his defense, just as he did the treatment the sheriff had accorded him after he had completed his business in Lordsburg and was arrested. But it was foolhardy – and useless, insofar as he was concerned – for Hayden to get himself at cross-purposes with Frank Slawson. It would accomplish nothing, might cause problems for the sheriff another day.

'Never mind,' he said, laying a hand on Hayden's shoulder.

'No, damn it – I aim to speak my piece!'

7

the lawman shouted, knocking Adam Gann's fingers aside. 'I'm going to keep tabs on you, Marshal. Happens the warden at Yuma's a friend of mine, and if Gann don't get there in decent shape – or don't get there a'tall – I figure to do something about it!'

Slawson stirred, picked up the pair of saddlebags he'd brought with him. Unbuckling one side, he took out a ten-foot length of chain with padlocks at each end.

'What's this all about, Sheriff?' he asked, pausing again to study the older man in his flat, expressionless manner. 'Why're you so riled up over this jailbird? He some kin of yours, maybe?'

'He ain't nothing to me, 'cepting he's a man.'

'An outlaw, convicted of murder,' Slawson corrected, handing one end of the chain to Gann. 'Put this around your middle – snug – and close the padlock.'

Gann shrugged, grasped the chain. Tall, dark-haired, light-eyed, by his own volition he had never been anything more than a cowhand who drifted about the frontier, working when and where he pleased. Now, however, that way of life had come to an end. Ten years in prison lay ahead for him, and with his customary stoicism, he had made up his mind to accept the bad cards luck had dealt him and make the best of it.

But that decision was suddenly undergoing

change, thanks to the actions and attitude of Deputy U.S. Marshal Frank Slawson, and a previously rejected idea of escaping into Mexico was becoming more appealing.

'You denying you killed that rancher?' Slawson continued.

'No,' Adam replied, looping the chain about his waist.

'Tight, I said,' the marshal reminded.

Gann's eyes flickered briefly. 'I aim to be comfortable,' he stated coolly, ignoring the lawman's order. There was an edge to his voice, a sullen defiance that, absent up to the moment when Slawson had struck him without reason, was now becoming apparent.

'I ain't claiming he didn't shoot J. W. Tucker,' Hayden said. 'Just trying to tell you he ain't no usual outlaw. Was a Saturday night brawl in a saloon, there in Paradise. Wound up in a shooting. Tucker got the worst of it.'

'For a fact,' Slawson said dryly, 'he got hisself killed.'

'Could just as easy been Gann, there, that caught the lead,' the sheriff said. 'Happened he was a mite faster'n Tucker. And anyways, folks what knows Tucker, knows what kind of a man he was. My guess is if that there trial had been held anywhere 'cepting Paradise, Gann would've been turned loose.'

'Maybe,' Slawson said. 'Way I hear it, Gann's always been a mite too quick and handy with his gun.'

Adam had completed the circle of chain about his waist, was closing it with the padlock. The marshal reached out, tested the slack in the ring of steel links. He nodded, satisfied.

'Ain't nothing wrong in that,' Hayden said. 'This here Tucker was an ornery sort, always spoiling for trouble and looking to pick a fight, 'specially if he could find somebody he could bully. Being big in the cattle-raising business, he seemed to think he was some kind of a god and could do and say anything he pleased and get away with it. He just picked the wrong man when he jumped on Gann.'

'Expect the judge was considering that when he passed sentence,' Slawson said. 'He could've hung him, or put him away for life. Instead he gave him only ten years.'

'Only ten years!' Hayden echoed. 'You know same as me what ten years in Yuma'll mean! A man'll come out, if he comes out, more dead than alive. His health's broke and he ain't worth a plugged copper – not to himself or anybody else.'

'That don't mean nothing to me, and it sure oughtn't to you,' Frank Slawson said, his voice rising with his temper. 'My job's to see that he gets to prison, not be fretting about how he's treated after he gets there. The law's the law, Sheriff, and you and me are paid to enforce it, not moon over the outlaws that break it. Gann, you got your belongings?'

Adam nodded slightly. He had sent all that he owned, with the exception of the clothing he was wearing, to his sister, along with what cash he had accumulated, reserving only a few dollars for himself; he'd have little need for money inside the high stone walls of Yuma Prison.

'Then let's move out. Long ride ahead of us.'

Gann turned to Dave Hayden, extended his hand. 'Obliged to you, Sheriff, for the favors.'

The lawman shook his head. 'Weren't no favors to it. Didn't do nothing no decent man wouldn't've done for you, under the circumstances.'

'I appreciate it, just the same.'

'Come on,' Slawson said, yanking on the chain and starting for the door. 'I ain't got–'

Gann, jerked off balance, recovered, and jaw set, planted his feet firmly and brought the marshal to an abrupt halt.

'Told you I'd give you no trouble,' he said quietly as Slawson, anger flaming in his eyes, wheeled to face him. 'You can forget it – and I'm serving notice on you right now – I don't figure on getting pushed around.'

'You'll take what I hand out!' Slawson snarled, again drawing his pistol. 'If I holler

Jump, by God, you better jump or I'll lay your head wide open – and this time I'll do a good job of it! Savvy?'

Gann folded his arms, considered the lawman with icy contempt. Despite the worn cord pants, the scarred stovepipe boots, faded plaid shirt, aged leather vest, and stained, wide-brimmed hat, he had the look of a man that it would be unwise to push too far.

'Lay a hand on me once more, Slawson, and all the bars go down. I'm not honing to go to Yuma, but I figured I would because I did what the law's sending me there for. But taking a hoorawing from you's not part of the deal. That's something you'd better savvy.'

The marshal stared at him unblinkingly. Then, 'You done talking?'

Gann made no audible reply, merely nodded slightly.

'Then let's go,' Slawson said, and trailing Adam Gann at the end of the chain, moved to the doorway and stepped out into the early morning sunlight.

'Luck,' Dave Hayden called, smiling at Gann.

'Thanks,' Adam replied. 'Same to you.'

Chapter 2

It was his own horse and saddle that were being provided for his use, Adam saw as they entered the livery stable at the end of the street. Such would be no doing of Frank Slawson, he was sure; it would be Dave Hayden endeavoring to make the long, hot ride to Yuma Prison as bearable as possible.

'They ready?' Marshal asked in his clipped, irritating way as the hostler came forward in the runway to meet them.

'Reckon they are,' the overalled man responded sourly. 'When'll I be getting paid?'

'First of the month, thereabouts,' Slawson said, and hanging his saddlebags over the skirt of the hull, eyed his horse, a tall black with a white blaze, critically. 'You find anything wrong with that left front leg of his? Like I said, he was favoring it some when I rode in.'

'Ain't nothing wrong other'n you been pushing him too hard without giving him no rest,' the stableman snapped. Then, 'You be bringing back my horse right soon? Figure he'll sell real quick, being a good animal like he is – Morgan blood and all. Sure would hate to lose out on a sale. Wouldn't've let you have him if the sheriff hadn't said it'd be a favor–'

'You'll get him back around the first of the month, too,' Slawson cut in, and taking the loose end of the chain, passed it through the hole in the bulge of his saddle and secured it with the second padlock. 'Can use a different horse if you're worrying about that one. Sure makes no difference to me.'

The hostler glanced at Adam, looked down. 'Naw, it's all right. Bay's already fixed to go. Was just trying to find out where I stand.'

'The government ever beat you out of anything?' Slawson demanded, testing his cinch.

'Nope, reckon not. Mostly because I ain't never done no business with it.'

'Well, you'll get your money and your horses right on time. I've rented plenty before this one,' the lawman said, turning to the pack horse and giving the load a shake to be certain it was secure. 'Everything here I told you to get?'

'Everything, including that stuff you toted in last night. Now, if you ain't believing me, why don't you just go through it?'

'No need,' Slawson said mildly. 'Wasn't nothing a man'd steal – it being only trail grub and such. Both of them canteens full?'

'Why don't you see for yourself?' the stableman shot back angrily, his face flushing.

For a reply the lawman stepped up to his

black and then to Gann's bay, each time hefting the metal water containers hanging from the horns. Satisfied, he again glanced at the pack horse, a solid-looking little gray, and then mounted his black.

'Climb aboard,' he said, jerking his head at Gann. 'Day's getting old.'

Adam turned to his horse, swung up onto the saddle, and settled himself, grateful to have the bay and his own gear under him. Slawson gave the chain a tug, drew in the slack to form a looping connection between them.

'I want you out in front of me all the time, jailbird,' the lawman said. 'And when I tell you to whoa, you whoa. Hear?'

Adam nodded, lifted the reins. It was three hundred and fifty miles to Yuma, across hills, flats, and burning desert; somewhere in between he'd have his chance.

'Let's go – right down the middle of the street. I want folks to see how the law treats killers.'

At the lawman's harsh command, Gann drummed on the ribs of the bay with spurless heels and clucked softly. The horse, long accustomed to his manner, stepped out obediently and turned into the roadway, now busy with Lordsburg citizenry going about their daily routines.

Adam could feel the eyes of many upon him as, linked to the marshal, chain glinting in the sunlight, they rode through the traffic. Slawson was getting great satisfaction in parading him before the town, but it was not bothering him; his time would come. Such antics on the part of Frank Slawson only increased his determination to make instant use of the very first opportunity that presented itself.

They reached the San Simon Valley near dark, pulled up alongside a creek that trailed down from the not too distant Whitlock Mountains, and made camp. It was a cool, pleasant place with ample shade, water, and firewood available.

'You'll be doing the cooking,' Slawson said in a matter-of-fact way, dismounting and removing the chain from his saddle. 'I'll see to the horses and such.'

Adam Gann scarcely heard. His attention was on the towering Chiricahuas to the south. The day's final sunlight was shining on their soaring peaks and the sky around them was filled with a soft, red glow.

'Jailbird – you hear me?'

Gann pulled himself away from the display of awesome beauty, a scene that never failed to stir him. Nodding, he came off the bay, wondering as he did if the lawman intended to take the chain from about his waist. In the next moment he had his answer; Slawson was instead fastening the opposite end to one of the trees that grew along the stream.

He was tethered – on a leash like a dog, he thought – and swore grimly. And then he shrugged it off. He should know he could expect nothing else from the marshal – why had he bothered to wonder?

Crossing to the gray, Adam removed the pack and dropped it to the ground. As the lawman began to lead the horses off to a grassy area a short distance below and near the creek, Gann dug into the provisions he found in a flour sack, located the spider, coffee pot, and other necessary articles. He turned then to the chore of preparing a meal of dried meat, potatoes and onions, warmed-over bread, and strong, black coffee.

By the time he was ready to cook, Slawson had gathered stones into a small, three-quarter circle, scooped out the loose dirt, and had a fire going. Saying nothing, Adam added water to the mixture in the frying pan and placed it over the flames. That done, he filled the pot from the clear, cold stream, added a handful of crushed beans, and maintaining a tightlipped silence, set it alongside the spider.

'Can see you've put your hand to cooking before,' Slawson said. He had chosen a place on the opposite side of the fire to squat, apparently being careful not to get too near his prisoner.

Adam only shrugged.

Little conversation had passed between

them since leaving Lordsburg, which was entirely to Gann's liking. A loner by nature, and now in the forced company of a man whom he had quickly learned to despise, he cared nothing about engaging in small talk.

'Hear it was that Turkey Track outfit over in the Wishbone country that you was working for when you killed that rancher.'

Gann said, 'Heard wrong. Been a year since I was there.'

Slawson drew out his tobacco and papers, began to roll a cigarette. 'Was a fellow name of Ed Gilroy that I knew. Recollect he punched cows for that same outfit. You know him?'

Adam stirred the contents of the frying pan, now beginning to simmer. 'No, guess not.'

'Was the foreman, seems.'

Gann made no reply. The stew was now bubbling busily and the lid on the coffee pot had begun to rattle as steam built up inside of it.

'Where'd you been when you shot that rancher at Paradise, if you wasn't at Turkey Track?'

'Montana.'

Slawson allowed smoke to trickle from his nostrils as he squinted at Gann. Back in the trees along the stream birds were chirping sleepily.

'You wanted by the law up there?' the

marshal asked bluntly.

Adam set the boiling coffee off to the side so that it might settle, pushed the frying pan to the rear of the rocks. Taking up the round loaf of bread he'd found in the supply sack, he tore off several chunks and placed them near the flames to warm. Only then did he put his cold attention on the lawman.

'I'm not wanted for anything – not there, not anywhere,' he said quietly.

'Except by the warden at Yuma pen,' Slawson said with a laugh. 'I aim to drop by there a couple of months from now, see how much they've changed you. Can bet they'll have took that cool-customer way of yours out of you, and you'll be begging for favors just like all the rest.'

Adam had no comment. He'd thought about Yuma, remembered all the tales he'd heard about the rocky, fortress-like establishment sweltering on a hill beside the Colorado River, and was anticipating the worst. But no matter how much he prepared himself he knew he'd never be ready for it – and doubted he would be able to accept what passed as a life there.

But since Lordsburg he had ceased to consider that possibility and with the passage of each mile that day his determination to escape at any cost became more resolute. If death lay ahead for him it was not to be at the hands of guards, with a grave in the shadow of prison walls, but somewhere in the gray-green hills or in the clean, wind-swept sand of the desert as the result of a futile attempt to escape from Frank Slawson.

'Grub's ready,' he said, jerking his head at the tin plates and cups.

The lawman flipped his dead cigarette into the creek, rose, and collecting the necessary items, helped himself to the stew and bread. Again settling himself on his heels, he put the heaped plate aside, poured a measure of coffee, all the while watching Gann closely as he spooned out a share.

'You know this country?' Slawson asked as they began to eat.

'Some,' Gann replied. He had crossed back and forth it several times besides working on three or four different ranches, but he didn't feel inclined to impart the information to the marshal.

'Then I reckon you know we've got a hell of a long, mean ride waiting for us – one that's going to take more'n a week.'

Gann reached for the salt sack. He had forgotten to season the stew. Slawson stared at him sullenly as he corrected the oversight.

'What I'm getting at,' the lawman continued, 'is we might just as well be sociable. Cuts down the hours, makes setting around the fire at night tolerable. Ain't nothing worse than having nobody to talk to.'

A hard half-smile cracked Adam Gann's lips as he glanced up at the lawman in disbelief. Slawson was telling him that they should be friends! After a moment he shook his head.

'Nothing we've got to say to each other, Marshal. Aim to let it stay that way. You keep your peace and I'll keep mine.'

Slawson's features colored. His eyes narrowed in the deepening shadows. His head bobbed briskly.

'All right, if that's how you want it, jailbird, that's how it'll be!'

'That's how I want it,' Gann said, and resumed eating.

Chapter 3

They rode out at sunup that next morning, grim and set and speaking only when the necessity arose. It was cool as they followed a westerly course across a hushed land bright with dew-freshened marigolds and silky, white thistles. Occasionally they caught a glimpse of jackrabbits, of perky, crested quail – some with chicks scurrying along in their wake; and once they saw a coyote slinking silently through the brush parallel with them.

As they progressed the day warmed, finally became intensely hot, and by the time they reached the Sulphur Springs country, not long before sundown, all signs of life – other than a half-dozen vultures circling high in the cloudless blue overhead – had vanished.

They made a dry camp, there being neither creek nor spring anywhere near, but it posed no problem. The canteens were better than half full, and by dark that next day they should have reached the San Pedro River, where they could replenish their supply and let the horses take their fill.

After the meal was over and they were sitting by the low fire – Gann sipping at his second cup of coffee, Slawson puffing at his pipe – Adam broached the question that had been nagging to be said ever since they left the San Simon Valley.

'We cutting up toward Tucson tomorrow?'

The lawman considered him suspiciously. 'You got a reason for wanting to go by there?'

Gann finished off the last of his coffee, set the cup aside. Pulling at the chain linking him to a nearby scrub tree, he shrugged.

'Nope, but it's plenty risky traveling this far south. Renegade Indians've been doing a lot of raiding along here – jumping pilgrims, even some of the ranchers.'

'Talk,' Slawson said indifferently. 'I've been across here half a dozen times, never had any trouble.'

'You've been lucky,' Adam said. 'I can think of half a dozen times that travelers – wagon trains, freighters, cowhands riding through – have been bush whacked.'

'Like I said, it's mostly talk. The Apaches are all peaceable.'

'The main tribes are. I'm talking about renegade hunting parties – bunches of young bucks that've split off the–'

'Don't reckon it's the Indians that're making you want to go by Tucson,' the lawman cut in. 'My hunch is you've got some friends hanging around up there that you figure'll give you a hand toward getting away from me.'

'Can't think of nobody up there I know,'

Gann said wearily, adding more wood to the fire. Darkness was now complete, and despite the withering heat that had prevailed during the day, a chill was now setting in.

'I didn't figure you'd be admitting it,' Slawson said dryly, knocking the dottle from his pipe by rapping it against the heel of his boot. 'Anyways, you can forget it. We ain't going nowheres near Tucson. I aim to keep moving due west till we come to the Barboquivaris, then slant north just a mite. Trail'll take us right into Yuma. I know because I've made the ride before.'

'Be a mistake,' Gann said stubbornly. 'Renegades are running loose all through here. You could've found that out from Hayden, or any other lawman in this part of the country, if you hadn't been too damn proud to ask!'

'The hell you say!' Slawson snapped.

Pipe stowed, he now produced tobacco and papers, and jaw set to an angry angle, proceeded to roll himself a cigarette. The chore quickly done, he took a brand from the fire, and cupping it with a hand, lit the slim, brown cylinder hanging from his lips.

'Expect I know this country better'n you!' he added.

'Doubt it,' Gann retorted.

'These here raids you heard about – it likely was just talk started by the army. They're spoiling for an excuse to move on the Indians, wipe them out.'

'Could be, but I'm doubting that, too. I've seen a few dead people that sure didn't die from talk. Anyway, good common sense will tell you we're taking a long chance in staying this far south.'

'What the hell difference does it make to you?' the lawman demanded. 'Considering where you're going, it sure oughtn't to matter to you what happens along the way!'

'You're right, Marshal,' Gann said with a half-smile. 'No sense in me worrying about my neck. I just wanted you to be sure you knew what you was getting yourself into.'

'Don't do me no favors!' Slawson snapped. 'And we ain't pointing toward Tucson, so you can forget about your friends' trying to take you away from me.'

'Suit yourself,' Gann said resignedly, and got to his feet.

Taking the chain in hand, he moved back from the fire, and picking up his blanket, crossed to a level place at the foot of a low cutback. Slawson watched him narrowly as he made his preparations in the shadowy darkness until he had settled down, and then, choosing a spot for himself on the opposite side of the camp – well beyond the length of Adam's restricting chain – he also retired.

For a while Gann lay awake staring up into the black arch bending over him. It was the time of month when the moon was small and the stars seemed extraordinarily low and bright.

So far there'd been no opportunity for an escape, but the determination was still there, stronger than ever. He had hoped to persuade the lawman to swing north, for the danger from renegade Apaches was very real despite Slawson's opinions to the contrary – and his own assurance that he had no friends waiting in or around the old mission settlement to aid him. But his efforts had failed and he would be forced to take his chances along with the marshal – which could result in the deaths of both of them should they run afoul of a party of renegades.

He fell asleep finally thinking, with wry humor, how that would nullify the need for an escape, and awoke early the next morning to find Frank Slawson already up and building a fire. Rising, Adam prepared a meal while the lawman got the horses ready, neither speaking during those minutes or while they were eating.

They were under way shortly after sunrise, following a line that took them even farther south than before, since it was necessary to skirt the Dragoon Mountains along the bleak formation's lower edge. They encountered no one, the country seemingly deserted except for them, and this strengthened Adam Gann's belief that renegade Apaches were prowling the land – something that everyone was aware of except Deputy U.S. Marshal Frank Slawson.

The heat had again risen to a punishing height by midday, and the late afternoon shadows were as welcome as was the sight of the tree-lined San Pedro River, which came into view just at dusk.

They halted beneath a large cottonwood standing at the edge of the stream, which ran clear and fairly deep although wide at this particular point, and set up camp. Brush grew thick around the small parklike area along with some of the lesser trees – paloverdes, and such. It was as fine a camping place as could be wished for, but neither man troubled to break silence and comment on the fact.

Immediately after dismounting, Slawson linked his end of Adam's chain about the cottonwood, and then, relieving the horses of their saddles, led them down to water a few yards below. Gann set to fixing the meal, making use of the ample supply of firewood at hand, and by the time the lawman had finished his chores with the horses – allowing them to drink and then picketing them on the lush grass – he had coffee ready and meat and potatoes frying over the fire.

'Reckon you'll admit now that talk about Apaches was all bull,' the marshal said, filling his cup with steaming, black liquid. 'Another whole day behind us and we ain't seen hide nor hair of any.'

Adam did not miss the faint note of triumph in Slawson's tone. 'Long way to Yuma yet,' he said. 'Still plenty of ground to cover.'

'Yeh, but we ain't likely to run into any now. For certain we won't soon's we get past the Mohawks.'

'Long way to them, too,' Gann said, mentally recalling the location of the range of low, smooth mountains on to the west.

'It ain't all that far,' the lawman said. 'This here coffee's like lye.'

Adam paused in the act of tearing off chunks of bread from the almost rock-hard loaf. Slawson still hadn't provided him with a large knife to use, and he refused to ask for one. He glanced at the marshal, smiled quietly; Slawson was in an argumentative mood.

'Be a good four days before we get there,' he said, ignoring the comment on the coffee. 'Maybe even more–'

Gann's words broke off, his eyes on the shadow-filled brush a hundred yards or so beyond the lawman. Slawson frowned, noting the abrupt change.

'What's the matter?' he asked.

'Saw something move down there in the chaparral.'

'Coyote, maybe a deer,' Slawson said, twisting about and throwing his attention to the darkening brush. 'Some bear around here, too. Animals always coming in about this time of day to water. I'll take my rifle–'

The marshal had come to his feet, turned, and was reaching for the weapon booted on his saddle lying nearby. He stiffened suddenly, froze.

'Indians!' he said in a raspy, breathless voice. 'Indians – surer'n hell!'

Chapter 4

Adam Gann reacted instinctively. Pivoting, he plunged into the river. As he struck the water, he came about, threw himself up against the bank. In the next moment, Slawson followed, and side by side they crouched in the cold stream.

'Give me a gun,' Adam said hoarsely as he strained to see the Indians through the closing darkness. He could see only slight stirrings in the brush.

'The hell with that,' Slawson replied tersely.

Gann swore in a low, frustrated voice. 'Damn it, if you aim to get out of here alive you'll need my help! Give me the rifle.'

There was no response from Slawson. Adam turned to face the lawman, saw the reason why; in his haste the marshal had failed to pick up the rifle, had only his pistol.

Gann swore again. 'You'll play hell doing much good against them with a six-gun,' he said, glancing about for a length of wood or anything else that would serve as a weapon. There was nothing suitable available.

'Unlock this chain so's I can move,' he directed. 'When they come to us, I'll make a run for the rifle.'

'I ain't about to,' Slawson said, hunching closer to the riverbank. 'Chances are they'll go on. Could be just a hunting party riding through, pulling up here for water. I'd be a damn fool was I to take that chain off you.'

'Except the truth is that you're not only a fool but that we're both dead, or good as. Is my word that I won't jump you or try running any good to you? I sure would like to be able to put up a fight. Not looking forward to letting a bunch of Apaches work me over.'

'Your word don't mean shucks to me,' Slawson said, eyes on the brush. 'Far as putting up a fight, I'll take care of that – and be looking out for you all the same time.'

The fire had dwindled to small, flickering tongues of flame. The horses were moving about restlessly, as if aware of impending trouble, and off along the river a duck called noisily. Adam, pressed tight against the damp, sandy bank of the San Pedro, continued to study the distant brush, little more than a dark blur in the weak light.

Perhaps the Indians were friendlier; maybe they would keep going once they'd watered their ponies, as Slawson thought – but Adam had his doubts. Apaches, even if not hostile, would have ridden into camp demanding a handout and casting about for something to steal.

'Expect you'll be plenty busy taking care of yourself,' Gann said.

31

He drew up slightly. There had been movement near a clump of mesquite close to the river, he thought. But he couldn't be sure. The shadows were now so deep it was almost impossible to see anything distinctly.

'If it comes down to that,' the lawman said, pulling back. 'I got a feeling they've moved on.'

'Don't think so. Was pretty sure I saw something move out there a bit ago.'

'Was probably the breeze stirring the brush around,' Slawson said, drawing himself fully upright.

In the tense hush Gann stared up at the lawman in disbelief and alarm. 'Don't be a fool! You're making an easy target of yourself!'

'Hell, they've gone,' Slawson said. 'And I sure don't aim to squat there in that water any longer'n I just have to.'

Pistol in hand, the marshal pulled himself up on the grassy bank and then stood erect, his squat shape silhouetted against the darkness beyond. Abruptly three gun shots shattered the quiet.

A yell spurted from the lawman's flared lips. His hat fell from his head as he spun half about. His fingers stiffened, releasing the pistol he grasped, allowing it to drop to the ground. Shouts came from the brush as he began to sink, and then, as he suddenly went over backward to drop half in, half out of the stream, figures began to dart from behind the trees and brushy growth and close in on the camp.

Gann whirled to the dead lawman. There was no hope of retrieving the fallen pistol or of getting the rifle, yards away and near the faltering fire. It didn't matter; he'd have no chance against the renegades. There were at least a dozen in the party.

Desperate, Adam thrust his hand into the lawman's shirt pocket – the one in which he thought Slawson kept the keys to the padlocks. The feel of cold metal against his fingertips encouraged him, sent hope racing through him. Taut, conscious of the unnerving yells of the braves drawing nearer, he tried the first of the keys. It was the wrong one. Evidently it fit the lock at the opposite end of the chain. Steeling himself, Adam applied the second key, gave it a turn. The padlock popped open.

Instantly, Gann freed himself from the loop encircling his body, and staying low, sank back into the water. The river was not deep enough for him to swim but did enable him to work his way, submerged, across to the other bank.

He had barely reached it and drawn himself in under an overhang of brush when the Apaches – several half-bent shapes approaching Slawson with care – appeared. It was evident they were not certain he was dead; also, they knew there had been two men in the camp and one was yet to be accounted for.

Tense, but well concealed, with only his head above water, Gann watched the renegades – at least a dozen in number – gather. In the failing light their half-naked bodies looked dull and dark as they began to search about for him in the brush and along the stream.

He didn't think any of them had reached the edge of the river in time to see him disappear under the overhang, or take note of the slight disturbance in the water that his movements had created, but he couldn't be sure. And then he became aware that one of the renegades had come down off the bank and was standing in the stream as he probed the opposite bank with a searching look.

Gann, refusing even to breathe, rode out the dragging moments. He doubted the Apache could actually see him – more than likely he was just suspicious – but as the man's unwavering stare held, Adam began to wonder.

Abruptly the brave turned and climbed, dripping, onto the bank. One of the Apaches had said something, calling him back, apparently. Gann sucked in a deep breath of relief, watched from behind his screen of foliage.

The party was splitting up. Two of the

renegades headed upstream, two going with the flow in an evident effort to find him. It had not occurred to them that he could have sought safety on the opposite side of the San Pedro, it would seem, unless, of course, they had kept their eyes on the bank at the far side of the river, and seeing no one emerge from the stream concluded he had not taken that route.

The remaining Apaches turned to Frank Slawson. Dragging the lawman up onto the grass, they began to rifle his body, taking everything on him including the deputy U.S. marshal's badge he was wearing. The brave claiming it laughed, pinned it to the seat of his breechcloth.

Finally satisfied there was no more to be found on the lawman, the Apaches drifted back to the center of the camp, began to paw through the gear and sacks of trail supplies. Shortly, the pair who had gone upstream reappeared. With considerable gesturing and guttural comment, they made known their failure to find anyone, and then joined in the pillaging.

One of the renegades appeared leading the horses. Shouts of approval went up as he brought the three animals into view. Immediately the Indians abandoned the litter made of the gear and supplies and concentrated on inspecting and admiring the horses. At that point the pair who had gone

35

downstream emerged from the brush.

Not pleased at being cut out of a share of the loot, they stood off to one side sulking for a few minutes. Then, walking to where the articles lay scattered about, began to move among them, touching some with the toe of their knee-high moccasins, occasionally stooping to pick up something, examine it, then throw it aside with a snort of disgust and anger.

Abruptly, the brave who seemed to be the leader of the party issued a terse command. The renegades, taking the horses, some of the food, the items removed from Frank Slawson's body, and his weapons, doubled back to the brush where Adam had first caught sight of them.

Shivering, Adam remained where he was, almost totally submerged in the cold water of the San Pedro. The renegades might return; they had ignored the saddles, most of the trail grub, and various bits of clothing that belonged to the lawman – and they just might have a camp of their own somewhere in the chaparral. He'd wait it out until he knew for certain they had either ridden on, or had settled down in the brush for the night.

It came to Adam Gann at that moment. With Frank Slawson dead he was free.

Chapter 5

'It's them Indians we seen – the same bunch,' Noah McLeod said, holding his old brass telescope to an eye and studying the commotion taking place along the river. 'They're after two men – white men.'

'Here, let me see.'

McLeod, a soft-spoken Virginian, was somewhere in his fifties, with cotton-white hair and a beard and mustache to match. He had piercing blue eyes, a ruddy face that gave the impression he was suffering from a severe case of sunburn, but in truth such was its natural color. Dressed in heavy-soled shoes, bib overalls, a faded, linsey-woolsey shirt, and a straw hat, he looked less the leader of a four-party wagon train headed for California than a farmer just in from the fields.

Frowning, he surrendered the glass to the younger man beside him – Rufus Enfield – and glanced about. Earlier he had spotted the Indians in the distance, had immediately swung wide of the area where they had halted in an effort to avoid them, finally bringing his charges to a stop on a slight hill well out of danger.

'We ought to help them.'

It was Daniel Price who spoke. Price was a few years older than McLeod, dressed much the same, and had small, dark eyes and iron-gray hair. Enfield was the younger brother of Price's wife, Flo, and was making the trip with them.

McLeod stirred, stroked his beard, and let his gaze touch the other members of the party: his wife, Beth, and their niece Sharon, whom they'd raised from infancy as their own daughter; big John Olson, his wife, Amanda, and their not-yet teen-age son, Willie; and the Ritters – Jim and his wife, Tillie, their three-year-old son, Jimmy Jr., and Charley, Jim's brother.

To go to the aid of the two men meant drawing the attention of the Indians to them – to their women and children, and the wagons – jeopardizing all. And like as not their stepping in would have little if any effect on the final outcome. The men of the train could muster only six or seven guns while there were at least twelve Indians, all well armed.

It was probably too late, anyway. There had been only that first quick rattle of gunshots and then silence. Such could mean that it was all over for the two white men. Noah turned to Enfield.

'What's it look like, Rufus?'

The younger man lowered the telescope, shook his head. 'Getting a mite dark down

38

there, an' seeing ain't so good. Hard to tell for certain, but I figure there's one of them dead and the other'n got clean away.'

Daniel Price stepped up, took the glass from his brother-in-law, trained it on the scene. 'One dead, all right,' he said. 'Laying half in the river. Can't see no sign of his partner. Noah, you sure there was two of them?'

'Reckon I am,' McLeod said a bit stiffly. 'Was both setting by the fire when I had me a look-see – right when we first pulled up. Anyways, if you look sharp you'll see two saddles off there to the left a bit.'

Price grunted. 'Yeh, I see them. Was two of them all right, and like Rufus says, one must've got away – but I expect they'll roust him out,' he added and passed the telescope back to McLeod.

'You think there's any use now of us sticking our nose in it?' Rufus asked. 'Fellow that got away could be a far piece off by now – and we sure can't help that dead man.'

'Would've been a mistake, anyway,' McLeod said. 'We got woman and kids to think about, and putting in our oar would've brought them Indians down on us in a hurry.'

Jim Ritter, a big, wide-shouldered blond with his young son in his arms, nodded approvingly. 'You figured right, Noah. Not only none of our business, but it would've sure been asking for trouble. If it's that same bunch of Indians we seen before, there's a bit party of them.'

'The same,' McLeod said, putting the glass to his eye again. 'Counted twelve both times. And the one that's the head of the outfit – the chief, I reckon he is – was riding a white horse with some feathers tied to its mane.'

'What're they doing now?' Price asked.

'Some of them are starting to look for the other fellow. Rest have dragged the dead man up onto the bank and are going through his pockets, helping themselves to whatever's on him.'

John Olson said, 'Like to have me a look, Noah. Ain't never seen Indians doing what they are.'

McLeod handed the telescope to the big man, smiled past him at Sharon and Beth. They had climbed down from the wagon seat, were now standing beside the team. Sharon smiled back and then put her attention on Rufus, who crossed to where she was.

Once the train reached California they would marry, he supposed – at least it was more or less understood that such would occur. It would be a good match. Rufus was young, strong as a bull, a hard and willing worker. He was bound to do well on a piece of land.

And Sharon was not one to shirk a duty, either. She'd make him a good wife – along with being a mighty fine looker, too. He hadn't noticed lately, being so preoccupied

with getting the train safely through dangerous country, but his girl had turned into a
beautiful woman – with her almost coal-
black hair, blue eyes, and full figure, which
at the moment was hidden under an old pair
of his work pants and a cast-off shirt.

Rose Sharon favored his brother Earl's
wife; she had been a beautiful woman, too,
but there was nothing else to her – all fluff
and laugh and nothing solid. In that way she
and her daughter differed vastly.

Olson's deep voice cut into Noah's
thoughts. 'Them savages are tearing up the
camp now. Done stripped that poor dead
man of what they want and are going
through their belongings. Fair makes my
blood boil to stand by, let them do that.'

Charley Ritter, silent up to that moment,
rubbed at his jaw thoughtfully. Also blond
and husky, he was two years older than his
brother Jim.

'This here's set me to wondering if we ain't
making a mistake,' he said. 'The country
ain't even half civilized, and coming out
here, bringing women and children–'

'California'll be all right – same with
Oregon if we decide to go on to there,' Price
said. 'Plenty of folks there – both places. It's
just the getting there that's chancey.'

''Specially when we ain't got nothing to go
by 'cepting an old map that ain't nowhere's
right,' Jim Ritter agreed. 'We ought to–'

'They're fixing to move on,' Olson broke in. 'The others've come back. Didn't find that fellow, seems, and they're looking over the animals. There's three of them. One was a pack horse, I expect.'

'Well, wasn't nothing we could do for the one that got killed,' Daniel Price said, biting a piece off his plug of tobacco. 'But seems to me it's our Christian duty to try and help the one that got away. Sure wouldn't be right to leave him down there afoot with no weapons or grub.'

McLeod nodded. 'Was what I was thinking, Daniel.'

'Sure can't help him if he ain't down there nowheres,' Rufus said, frowning.

'Expect he'll be around close – hiding out,' Noah said. 'We'll set tight until them Indians've gone for sure. Then we'll see what we can do. They still there, John?'

'Fixing to leave right now,' Olson said, and returned the glass to McLeod.

Noah leveled the telescope on the small clearing. It was almost too dark to make out what was taking place now, but he could see the Indians leading the three horses back toward a dark band of brush. The belongings of the two men still lay scattered about – grub sacks and a box or two looming up white in the deep shade.

'They gone?' Daniel Price asked. 'That other fellow could be bad hurt and needing help. We ought–'

'We best wait,' McLeod said. 'When I see them savages off a mile or so, and moving on, then we can go down there.'

Chapter 6

Gann, trembling from the cold water, remained hidden under the overhang of the bank. He could hear no sounds other than the croaking of a frog somewhere below him and the distant moaning of a dove. Darkness was almost total now, particularly among the trees and in the brush, but there was still light in the sky.

He was in a hell of a fix. That thought came to him abruptly. No horse, no gun, more or less surrounded by desert – by any reasoning he was caught between a rock and a hard place. Even so, he reckoned he was lucky; he no longer was a prisoner on the way to ten hard years of servitude in one of the worst penitentiaries in the country, and he had managed to survive a renegade Indian attack that had cost the life of the man with him.

But he'd make out, somehow. The Apaches had ignored most of the grub and both canteens, and Tucson couldn't be too far – somewhere around a hundred miles he judged, raking his mind to place his exact location.

True there could be settlements, as well as

ranches and homesteaders, nearer, but he had no idea in which direction; and a man on foot in the desert had better know where he was going before he started out, otherwise he could wander fruitlessly for days until the murderous heat and exhaustion felled him. He was certain where Tucson lay – west and a bit north; striking out for it would involve no risk.

The dry rattle of brush reached Adam Gann. He pulled back farther into the cove beneath the overhang as tension began to build within him suddenly. The sound had come from behind him, not from across the stream where he and Slawson had pitched camp. More Apaches? He doubted it; their approach would be quieter.

The noise became louder – the crackle of dead branches, the thud of heavy shoes or boots, finally men's hushed voices. He could be little better off, their not being Indians, Adam realized. It might be a party of busters, plentiful in the area – men who had failed in their quest for gold or silver, and in so doing lost everything and become outlaws, preying on travelers as did the renegade Apaches.

If so, they wouldn't get much from him if they found him. A few dollars was all he carried, and of course there were the two saddles over in the camp. That evoked a thought. They would not be aware that

Slawson was a federal marshal unless some member of the party had been acquainted with him. The Apaches had stripped Slawson of his badge, papers, cash, and all else. To them the lawman would be just an ordinary pilgrim. To further his own freedom and welfare he need only keep quiet about Frank Slawson's true identity. If he–

'You reckon he could've got away?'

The speaker was directly above the overhang, so close that the soft-edged, southern-accented voice startled Adam Gann. They were looking for him all right.

'Them savages could've caught the poor devil after they left here.' It was a different man.

'Don't think so. Was keeping the glass on them. He's hiding around here somewheres.'

There were at least three in the party, Gann concluded, but there was no way of telling who or what they might be. Tense, doing his utmost to control his shivering, he waited.

'Maybe.' It was yet another voice. 'Man smart enough to fool them savages would be smart enough to get clean out of here.'

'Or just the opposite – he'd be smart enough to stay well hid till he was plumb sure nobody was around.'

'Well, if he is and sees us taking care of his partner, I expect he'll show hisself. He'll figure we're friends. Let's get over there and get the dead one buried.'

'A bit dark to be doing anything without a light.'

'Daniel's brought a lantern. Won't take long, all of us using spades.'

There was a splash in the water to his left. Adam turned slightly under the overhang, put his attention toward the sound. He was fairly sure now the men were not outlaws and meant no harm; like as not they were pilgrims passing through who happened to witness the Apache attack.

'Sure suits me. Sooner we get back to the wagons, the better I'll feel. Don't like leaving the women and young'uns.'

'Ritter's with them. They'll be all right.'

Adam Gann took a deep breath. They were pilgrims – members of a wagon train. Gathering his cramped legs, he moved out from beneath the overhang, drew himself upright. Ahead he could see dark shapes wading through the knee-deep water, five in all, plus one who had apparently been left back in their camp – Ritter, the one with the deep-south accent had called him. It wasn't a very large train; they were taking a big chance crossing Apache country.

'Over here,' he called softly.

The men paused, wheeled. They were startled but showed no alarm. For several moments they only stared at Gann as water drained from him in a dozen rivulets, and

47

then one spoke.

'You the dead man's partner – the one them savages was hunting for?'

'That's me. Name's Adam Gann.'

'Good. Wasn't sure if they'd caught you or you'd struck off down the river. Where was you and your partner headed?'

'West,' Adam replied, moving forward to join them. 'You?'

'California,' one of the men, much younger than the others, replied. 'Maybe even Oregon. Depends on how things are.'

'Guess it's all in what you're figuring to do. If it's farming, I'd say you'd be better off in Oregon, excepting in the northern part of California–'

'What the hell are we standing here in the water jawing for?' the man holding the lantern demanded impatiently. 'Can talk later. Let's get the job of burying that fellow done. Them savages just might take a notion to come back, and we sure don't want to be anywheres around.'

'Daniel's right,' the one with the thick accent said, moving on toward the bank. 'We're aiming to bury your partner, Gann. After that we'll see what we can do for you.'

The group moved to the shore, climbed up onto the grassy land. At once all crossed to where Slawson lay and began to dig hurriedly. Adam squatted beside the lawman.

'Ain't no use going through his clothes.

48

Them savages took everything he had.'

Gann nodded. Reaching beyond the rigid body, he retrieved the marshal's hat and placed it on his own head. The one he'd worn had fallen into the river when he'd plunged over the bank, and floated off downstream.

'What was his name?'

Gann gave the question quick thought as the spades bit steadily into the sandy soil. The truth wouldn't matter, he guessed, and a lie could lead to trouble later.

'Frank Slawson,' he said, and let it drop there. There was no point in complicating matters by revealing that the dead man was a deputy U.S. marshal – at least not right at that moment.

'I'll scrape his name on that piece of sandstone there,' one of the pilgrims – a tall, rawboned man with hair that showed light even in the rapidly closing darkness – said. 'You know how old he was?'

'Sure don't.'

'Guess it won't make any difference,' the blond said. 'Can put down the date he was killed. Anybody know what today is?'

The grave was near finished: a narrow trench six feet in length, no more than three feet deep.

'All you'll need, John, 's the year.' The heavily accented voice of the man who was evidently the leader of the train, was low.

'Just put 1878.'

The big man turned away, and picking up a fair-sized rock, placed it in a level position on the ground before him. Then, taking a bit of steel from a pocket, he began to etch the information obtained onto the bit of soft stone.

'You want the lantern, John?' the one called Daniel asked. It had not been lit, the glow of stars and moon furnishing sufficient light for the digging of Slawson's grave.

'No, can see all right,' John answered.

'Gann, you want to say something over your friend.'

Adam turned. The marshal's body was in the trench, and two of the men were hastily covering it over. As far as he was concerned the lawman could be put down and forgotten, but he supposed for appearance's sake he'd best make some sort of remark.

'Didn't know him too well,' he said as the grave, full now, became a long mound. 'He was a good man, honest far as I know, and I reckon there'll be somebody somewhere who'll miss him.'

Gann paused, stepped back. He was trembling considerably from the cold imparted by his wet clothing. He felt the eyes of the men upon him, looked down. And then the voice of Daniel came to him.

'God rest his soul. Amen... Now, what about your gear? You don't figure to leave them saddles, do you? And there's quite a bit of grub, and your blankets and canteens–'

'Like to take it all,' Adam said, thinking ahead. He would be needing a horse; maybe he'd be able to trade Slawson's saddle for one. As far as the food and the pans and such were concerned, he'd give all of it to the pilgrims as a sort of payment for bailing him out of the tight spot they'd found him in.

'Then let's gather it all up and get out of here,' the leader of the wagon train said. 'Take everything. We'll sort it out and let Gann throw away what he ain't wanting later. You boys all done with the burying?'

'All done, Noah,' one of the two engaged in smoothing the dry soil of the grave replied. 'Can use that headstone now, John.'

The big blond stepped up, the bit of sandstone with carving on its smoother side in his thick hands. Squatting, he cupped out a hollow at one end of the grave and set the marker in place, taking a few moments to tamp the loose soil firmly about it.

'Done all we can for him, I reckon,' he said, rising and glancing at Adam.

Gann nodded. 'Obliged to you – all of you,' he said, 'but like a couple of you've mentioned, we best get out of here quick. Never can figure what an Apache might do.'

'Man's right,' Noah said. 'Let's go.'

Chapter 7

Carrying the two saddles and other items, Gann, in company with the wagon train men, stepped back into the stream, waded across, and gained the opposite bank. There they cut left and struck off through the trees and brush for a low hill looming vaguely in the near distance.

Shortly Adam, the chill of the water now fading as his clothing dried, saw the arched, white tops of the vehicles. They had been halted near the base of the rise, the point from which the members of the party had watched the Apaches, he assumed, glancing back. There would have been daylight then, and from their higher position they would have had an excellent view.

Sudden questions pressed forward in Gann's mind. Could they have seen the renegades remove the star from Frank Slawson's body? Could they have noticed the chain with which the lawman had secured him to the tree? Had they watched him take the padlock key from the man's pocket and free himself?

If so, no mention had been made. It seemed unlikely. Having been witness to such, and thus being made aware that Gann was a prisoner of Slawson, whom they would immediately assume to be a lawman even had they failed to see his badge, they would not have been so willing to help.

A dark shape, rifle in hand, materialized from between the four wagons, drawn into a half circle, and came forward slowly.

'It's us, Charley,' Noah said. 'We found the fellow, brought him along.'

The man on guard halted. 'Figured it was you all, but was aiming to be sure. Heard you coming for quite a piece.'

'Everybody all right?' Daniel asked, the still-dark lantern swinging from his hand.

'Sure are. Kids are sleeping in the wagons. Womenfolk are still up – waiting. Got coffee ready. Built the fire in that hollow next to the bluff. Don't think it can be seen.'

Noah said, 'We couldn't coming up from the river. Don't know about the other way.'

'Was careful to blind it,' Charley said as they reached the first of the wagons. Circling by it, they entered a shallow bowl where several women were standing around a small fire.

Gann lowered the saddle he was carrying on a shoulder to the ground. The man toting Frank Slawson's followed suit, while Noah and the others, each with bits of camp gear and salvaged food, relieved themselves of their loads.

Nodding to Adam, Noah said, 'Expect we best start off by telling you who we are. My name's Noah McLeod. Them two ladies there by that rock are my wife, Beth, and our daughter – actually our niece – Rose Sharon. We all call her Sharon.'

Both women – Beth, large, dark-haired, and capable-looking, and Sharon, probably in her early twenties and strikingly beautiful, even in the weak firelight – smiled in a friendly fashion.

The older woman said, 'You are all wet. Best you get in close and dry out.' She had a deep, full voice.

The men obediently edged farther into the hollow. Noah gestured at the youngest man in the party.

'He's Rufus Enfield, and standing next to him's Daniel Price. Lady in the calico dress is Daniel's wife, Flo – and Rufus's sister.'

'John Olson – he's the one that fixed up the marker for your partner's grave – the big fellow there. That's Amanda, his wife, standing next to him. They've got a son, Willie. Expect he's in the wagon sleeping.'

'Just what he's doing,' Amanda Olson said, and then laughed. 'Leastwise he'd better be.'

'Charley Ritter's the fellow who come out to meet us. Oversized man with him's his brother Jim. Charley ain't married. That little gal you see between them belongs to Jim. Name's Tillie. They've got themselves a son, too. Three years old or thereabouts. Reckon he's asleep, too.'

'Sure is,' Tillie assured him.

Noah paused, glanced about. 'Seems that covers everybody. Now, folks, this is Adam Gann. Was his partner them savages killed. He managed to get away and hide out till they'd gone. Lost about everything excepting his saddle and blankets, and some grub and cooking pans.'

Everyone pressed forward, shook Adam's hand, murmuring words of congratulations on his escape, expressions of condolences over his loss, and bidding him welcome.

'We buried his partner – fellow name of Frank Slawson,' McLeod went on. 'Figured we could find a place with us for him till he could make other arrangements.'

'Where was you and your partner headed?' Charley Ritter asked as the women began to pass tin cups filled with steaming coffee among them.

'West,' Adam replied without giving it much thought.

Gann took a swallow of the hot, black liquid. It was chicory, he saw, but it tasted good, finished nullifying the chill the water of the San Pedro and the cool night had produced.

McLeod said something to Price in a low tone, repeated it to Olson and Jim Ritter. At their nods, he turned to Adam.

'You know this country?'

Gann's shoulders stirred. 'Guess you could say I do. I've crossed it a few times.'

'We're going to California – already told you that I guess – but we're strangers and we ain't sure we're taking the best way.'

Gann took another sip of the chicory. He was watching Sharon, struck by her beauty and easy charm. So also was Rufus Enfield. The younger man was exhibiting a considerable amount of possessiveness to which the girl was responding. Apparently there was something between them.

Adam brought his attention back to Noah McLeod and the words he'd spoken, smiling wryly. 'You took a big risk cutting through Apache country.'

Noah wagged his head. 'Just what I'm getting at. We plain don't know no better. Fact is, we'd been told the army had settled the Indians down and we wouldn't have no trouble. Was bad information.'

'Some,' Gann agreed. 'Tribes are all friendly around here now, but now and then a bunch of young bucks will jump the reservation and stir up trouble. Was what that party was back there along the river. If you'd done your traveling farther to the north, like most wagon trains do, chances are you'd not even see an Indian.'

The women had pulled off to the opposite side of the fire, talking quietly among themselves. Adam could see Sharon McLeod was eyeing him, either curious or interested, he couldn't be sure. A quick thought moved through him; if he was going to stay with the train, and the girl did show more than casual interest in him, he'd best discourage her immediately regardless of how much she appealed to him. He had nothing to offer a woman.

Ahead of him lay a life of dodging the law, of hiding below the border in Mexico, of living in the shadows. Anyway, it could only be curiosity that Sharon was feeling.

'Now that's the kind of advice and help we're needing,' McLeod declared. The other men were standing around him as if to back up all he was saying. 'We're going to make you an offer, Gann, and hope you'll be taking it. We want to hire you on as a guide to get us to California.'

'You're stranded here,' Daniel Price added. 'You ain't got a horse and no weapons. We can fix you up with both, along with eating regular.'

'We can come to a meeting of the minds on what it'll be worth to you,' McLeod said, 'same as we can on what it will to us.'

'And that ain't mentioning that it'll be a mighty big favor to us,' Olson said, 'because we'll all rest easier knowing we got a man along who won't let us get ourselves into a fight.'

'And who probably knows a better trail than the one we're following,' Price said. 'What do you think?'

Adam Gann stared off into the night. It was more than he could have hoped for – a way out of the bind the Apaches had put him in, and further escape from Yuma. He could stay with the McLeod party until they reached the Colorado River, where California began, and then head down into Mexico.

Once there, and safe from the reach of the law, he'd get word off to Tim Aubrey, owner of the Turkey Track ranch up near the Wishbone Mountains, let him know what had happened during his absence and ask him to have a talk with the governor. Aubrey had told him when he quit that if he ever needed a favor to get in touch. The rancher should be back from his extensive vacation in the East by then.

It would all work out fine, assuming he didn't encounter any lawmen searching for him in the miles that still lay ahead to California, and that wasn't likely. Too, it wouldn't be all one-sided – his way; the McLeod wagon train needed him as much as he did them, and that cut the edge of the deception he would have to practice to some extent.

'Suits me,' he said, and extended his hand first to McLeod, as the leader, and then to each of the others in turn. When it was over, he turned back to Noah.

'Don't want to start right off giving orders,' he said, 'but it'll be smart to move on, find a better place to camp. Can just about bank on them Apaches coming again, and when they see somebody's been there, taken the stuff they left–'

'Yeh, the saddles,' Rufus Enfield cut in. 'Why didn't they want them?'

'Won't use them,' Adam explained. 'Figure they weigh down their horses too much. Surprised, though, they didn't take time to cut off the straps. Always after leather.

'Thing is, when they see the hulls are gone along with the rest of the stuff, and that Slawson's been buried, they're going to start looking around for who did it. We'd best have a few miles between us and them when that happens.'

'Amen,' Daniel Price said. 'Let's get moving.'

Chapter 8

McLeod caught at Adam Gann's arm as everyone turned away. 'That's my wagon there – with the new red wheel. Can throw your stuff in the back and ride with my women and me. Having somebody to spell me off in the driving will be mighty nice.'

'You ain't hardly got room enough for all your belongings now, Noah,' Olson said, overhearing. 'I can put one of them saddles in my rig. Come daylight we can shift things around a bit, make a place for all.'

McLeod nodded, glancing about as he kicked dirt over the fire. Waiting until John Olson had climbed to his seat, he called: 'Everybody ready?'

Replies in the affirmative came from the hooded wagons. 'Want you all to take it slow and real careful,' he continued. 'We ain't used to night traveling, and this here's plenty rough country. I don't want no horses hurt or wagons turned over. Be mighty easy for it to happen.'

'I'll be walking out ahead,' Gann said, reaching for the lantern hanging from the side of the vehicle. 'You be at the head of the line?'

'Way it's been,' Noah replied, pulling himself up onto the seat. Adam could see the faces of Sharon and Beth in the darkness beneath the arch as they waited to get underway.

Gann handed the lantern up to McLeod. 'Light it. Got my matches wet,' he said. 'Then follow me. I'll break trail for you.'

McLeod grunted his approval, and striking a match, lit the lantern's wick, reset the globe, and passed it down to Adam. Rising, he looked to the others.

'Gann'll be lighting the way for us,' he called in a soft voice. 'Want you all to keep up close.'

Adam had already moved out in front of McLeod's team and was peering ahead. There was little help coming from the sky, the moon being weak and the stars partly veiled by thin, drifting clouds. But it appeared the route wouldn't be too rough if he kept the wagons along the foot of the hill where they had halted, and pointed for what appeared to be a grove a short distance away.

From there on it was only a guess as to what they would get into; he was not familiar with the area, having done his traveling more to the north when he crossed the territory, but he seemed to recall that the country was mostly low, barren hills, rocky washes, and wide, sandy arroyos interspersed with flats.

That, however, was something he could

better determine in daylight. The task facing him now was to get the McLeod train a safe distance from where he and Frank Slawson had been attacked by the renegade Apaches.

Swinging the lantern back and forth as a signal, Gann moved on, walking slow so as to not get too far ahead of the lumbering wagons. It was easy going, the grade being gentle and only occasionally cut by shallow washes.

Reaching the foot of the rise, Gann veered due north, now heading directly for the grove and its end, to his left. There would be good camping places once they gained the trees, a dark band that marked the course of the river, but he was reluctant to stop immediately upon arriving there. McLeod and the others, in taking him on as their guide, were in effect placing not only their trust but their lives and those of their families in his hands. He couldn't afford to make a mistake.

The edge of the grove would be little more than a mile from the camp where the renegades had struck, and that simply wasn't enough distance; it would be easy for the Apaches, visiting the scene of the attack, to swing out, search about until they found the prints of the wagon wheels, and follow. He'd best do something about that, too, he realized, rubbing at his whiskery jaw.

Adam glanced back, slowed. He'd pulled away from the wagons a bit more than he liked, but he was still near enough to make out Noah McLeod hunched on the seat of his vehicle with Sharon beside him. The others, observing McLeod's instructions to not lag, were close behind.

Gann turned his eyes again to the country ahead. The dark wall of growth that indicated the presence of the river was now due south and no more than a quarter mile distant. This would be his best opportunity to wipe out the signs of their passage, he decided, and swung toward the stream, hoping as he did that the San Pedro would be as wide and shallow in this section as it was on below.

Coming to its edge, he grinned tightly. He would be able to put his plan in effect. Raising the lantern, he halted McLeod a dozen yards short of the stream and dropped back to talk.

'Like for you to cut left and drive down into the water,' he said, pointing to an opening in the brush crowding the river's banks. 'When you get in, drive on for a bit, then turn around, head back up stream – but don't get out of the water until I give you the word.'

McLeod stroked his beard thoughtfully. At his side Sharon, her face a pale oval in the silvery light, considered Adam with a frown. It was the former who spoke.

'Not sure I know what you're aiming to do–'

Adam glanced to his right as Price and

Rufus Enfield hurried up, questions on their faces.

'Being sure we don't leave any tracks for those renegades to follow,' Gann said, and went over the plan again for the benefit of Daniel Price and his brother-in-law. 'We head into the stream like we're going south, then we double back north.'

'Sure – I understand,' Price said. 'Water'll wash out our tracks except where we went down into the river.'

Rufus, smiling at Sharon, said, 'How about where we come out?'

'We'll stay in the riverbed as long as we can,' Gann said. 'I'll keep in front with the lantern same as I've been doing. If I come to a place where the wagons can't make it, I'll call a halt and we'll clear the way. If we can't do that, then we'll pull up onto the bank.'

'Do you really think those Indians will follow us?' Sharon asked.

Adam glanced at her. He liked the sound of her voice. 'Yes'm – we can just about plan on it. And they won't have any trouble finding the wagon wheel tracks back where you stopped, and where we came off the hill. Trick now is to lead them off into the wrong direction and start them hunting us somewhere else.'

'It's being smart,' Daniel Price stated. 'I sure never would've thought of doing it myself.'

'None of us would, I expect,' McLeod said. 'We just ain't used to having to do things careful like this. Rufus, it'll probably be a good idea for you to go along with Adam, give him a hand in case he needs it.'

Enfield shrugged, showing little enthusiasm for the idea, but he nodded and said, 'All right. Wait'll I get me a lantern,' and turned away.

'How much longer you figure it'll be before we can pull up, make camp?' Price asked. 'It's been a long day. Folks are plenty tired – animals, too.'

'Couple of hours ought to do it,' Gann said. 'Just want to play it safe.'

'Don't think I'm kicking!' Price said hastily. 'We're all indebted to you for taking over and looking out for us. It's just that the others'll be wanting to know and I'd like to have an answer for them.'

'I'll get you to a camping place soon as I can,' Adam assured the man and came about as Rufus Enfield, carrying a lighted lantern, returned.

Nodding to McLeod, Gann waited until Price had resumed his seat and then made a forward motion with his free hand.

'Just follow me. Want to make this look as good as we can,' he said, and with Enfield at his side, started for the river.

Chapter 9

'North?' Charley Ritter echoed in a puzzled voice. 'We ought to keep traveling west.'

It was well after dawn, and the men were gathered about the cook fire drinking the last of the chicory before moving on. Gann had kept the wagon train in the river that previous night for a long three hours before he had become convinced it was safe to go ashore and make camp. As a result the party was late getting organized for the day's journey.

'North,' Adam repeated. 'The sooner we get out of Indian country, the better I'll like it.'

'Ain't there Indians north of here, too?' Price asked. 'Somebody told us we'd like as not be running into them all the way to California.'

'You've been told right, but the only ones that get out of hand now and then are from the tribes south of here.'

'Is it going to be any farther – swinging north like you're wanting to do?' Noah Mc-Leod wondered.

'Not much,' Gann replied, beginning to have doubts as to the wisdom of accepting the job as guide for the party of pilgrims. If it was going to be necessary to explain every move he made, in detail, and to the satisfaction of each member of the wagon train, then the road to California would be a mighty long one!

'How about the desert? We be able to dodge it if we go the road you're talking about?'

Adam shook his head in reply to John Olson's question. 'No way I know of to get where you're headed without crossing the desert. The Mohave, as it's called, lies between us and California, and there's no way of getting around it. Besides, we've got a lot of hot, dry country yet in Arizona before we get to it.'

'Worse'n what we've already come over?' McLeod asked.

Gann cast an impatient glance to the east, shrugged. Might as well accept it; they were going to get a late start.

'I don't know where you're from, but I don't think you could've crossed anything as bad as what we've got ahead.'

'We're from Virginia all of us,' McLeod said. 'Came down from Tennessee and Arkansas and into Texas and New Mexico, and on to here – Arizona.'

'Can figure that was easy traveling. Now, I sure don't want to scare you, but the worst is still out in front, starting about today, and after looking over your outfit I ain't sure you're in shape to try it.'

Jim Ritter swore softly, tossed the last of his chicory into the dying fire. The others exchanged frowning glances. On beyond them the women were getting things ready to move out. One of them – Olson's wife, Adam thought – was singing a hymn in a low, sweet voice as she went about her work.

'What makes you say that?' Price demanded, anger in his tone. 'We got the best wagons we could buy, and brought along only what we just had to have.'

'For one thing, you're short of horses. All you've got is your working teams and two extras.'

'Mine,' Ritter said, a bit proudly.

'Ought to be a spare team for each wagon. Surprises me some that you've come this far without running into trouble – using the same horses every day.'

McLeod scratched at his beard. 'Was a couple of times when we needed fresh teams, all right,' he admitted in his soft-edged voice. 'But fact is, Gann, none of us 'cepting the Ritters could afford to buy extra horses. Took all we could scrape up to make the move, and still have a little left to settle the land and buy seed.

'But we're listening to you and taking your word for what's got to be done – never was no hand to hire on an expert and then not let him do his job.'

'We've come this far,' Price said, 'and we sure ain't turning back now, no matter what.'

'That's right,' Olson said, laying his hand on Price's shoulder. 'And Noah's right, too. We're leaving it up to you to do what's best for us, and to get us to California. We ain't interested in settling around here, or anywhere else.'

Gann nodded slowly, stared out over the flats and low, bubble-like hills stretching endlessly before them. High overhead half a dozen vultures were soaring in broad circles, and back along the river, a quarter mile distant, a mountain lion squalled for some reason, causing all to pause and look toward the source of the eerie sound.

'I'll get you there,' he said. 'We may have to take it slow in places, and we'll all need to work together, but I reckon it can be done.'

'If it's going to be all that hard, how about going through Nevada?' Charley Ritter suggested. 'I recollect somebody along the way claimed it was a good route.'

'Still have desert to cross, and, if I'm remembering right, there's plenty of mountains.'

'Then we sure don't want to risk that road with no extra horses,' John Olson said. 'What about this way we're taking – there any towns along the way? I'm getting a mite low on grub. Expect the others are, too.'

'There'll be a few settlements on past Tucson. Can stock up at one of them.'

'What about Tucson? Been told it was a fair-sized town.'

'It is, but going there would cost us some extra miles, and a lot of time. We've got to follow along those hills over to the right – the Dragoons, folks call them – and then circle the Catalinas. They'll be showing up on your left in a couple of days. Once we're past them, we'll head west again.'

'That where the desert begins?' Price asked.

'Not the Mohave. We've got the rest of Arizona territory to cross, which means about most of it, before we reach the Mohave. But there's plenty of heat and dry between here and there. May be a good thing, too. It'll sort of get us, and the horses, ready for the real desert.'

'Then when will we reach this – this Mohave?' Ritter wondered.

Gann gave that thought, lightly scrubbing the whiskers on his burned features as he did. From the front of McLeod's wagon he saw that Sharon, now wearing a dress, had paused to hear his answer.

'Rate we'll be moving I'd guess it'll be nine, maybe ten days, figuring we don't have to pull up and lay over for some reason.'

'Then, from there, how much longer till we get to California?'

'Well, the Mohave's mostly in California, but there's some of it lapping into Arizona – which has a'plenty of its own laying alongside–'

'Then how'll we know when we get to California?'

'There's a river – the Colorado. It marks the line. We'll be heading for a town called Flatrock that sets on the east bank. There's a ferry there that'll take you across.'

'And into California,' Olson said with a deep sigh. 'Seems like we've been headed there for years!'

'Still a fair piece from there to where you aim to end up,' Adam cautioned. 'Once you're on the other side of the Colorado, you drive due west till you come to the ocean.'

'Now, how far's that?' Olson asked in a falling voice.

'Maybe a week's traveling, about half of it desert. But you'll be in good shape once that's behind you. Can start heading north for where you want to go, through mighty fine country – warm but nothing like the desert. You'll be following along the ocean all the way.'

'Could be we can pull up, stop, if we find good farming land instead of going on.'

'You'll see plenty of places to stop this side of Oregon,' Gann said. 'I've made the trip a couple of times. I remember there being a lot of fine-looking country... We about ready to move out?'

McLeod fumed, glanced over the half circle of wagons. The women and children were not in sight, and all appeared set to go.

'Reckon we are.'

'Best we get started, then,' Adam said, and paused as McLeod beckoned to him.

'Mind doing some driving for me today?' the older man asked. 'Them miles in that river last night, bumping and jerking me around, sort of took the sap out of me. My wife thinks it'd do me good to rest up.'

'Sure – glad to.'

'Fine. I'll do my riding in the back with her. Rose Sharon can set up on the seat with you, keep you company. I don't reckon Rufus'll mind. They're sort of promised to each other, in case you didn't know.'

Gann suppressed the pleasure that had surged through him. It was not because of what Noah McLeod had said concerning Rufus Enfield and the girl, but simply that there was no future for him with her or any woman. That was a fact he must not allow himself to forget.

Chapter 10

Sharon settled herself on the wagon seat and spent a moment or two tucking a stray lock of dark hair back into place under her bonnet. She had changed from her usual sturdy garb to a pale blue company dress, an act that had drawn immediate and critical attention from the other women – all of which she had blithely ignored.

She knew the low-cut blue with its lace trim was far from suitable under the circumstances, but she'd had an urge to wear it, and Beth, reading her mind and always one to understand, had arranged for her to ride beside Adam Gann by insisting that Pa take the day off to rest.

She felt a bit wicked about the whole thing and was unsure in her own mind just what had brought about the sudden impulse to shine up to Adam Gann, as Pa would have put it. Up to only a few short hours ago she had been perfectly content to go on living her life as always insofar as men were concerned, paying no particular mind to their attentions although they were flattering and made her feel good.

And of course there was Rufus – good old

reliable, always-right-there Rufus. She supposed it could be said there was an understanding of sorts between them, but actually it had never been put to words; it was that Rufus assumed, as did Pa and Beth and all the others, that they would eventually marry. She had gone along with it, neither affirming nor denying but just tolerating the impression and allowing it to survive mostly because there had been no alternative.

Maybe that was what had induced her to make changes in herself – a bit of rearranging where her hair was concerned, prettying up her face a bit, and donning the blue dress. Beth had thought it a good idea, and Beth – she had insisted on being called by her given name rather than 'Aunt' or 'Mother' or the customary 'Ma', from the time that she and Noah had taken her in – always knew what was right and what was wrong.

'Don't lose sleep over what other folks think,' she'd said. 'It's you that'll have to satisfy yourself. If it's not right you'll feel it; if it is you'll not even wonder, you'll just know it.'

Beth had paused thoughtfully after that, and after watching Sharon for a few moments as she dressed, had said, 'The stranger's kind of taken your eye, hasn't he? That's why you want to wear your party dress.'

Sharon had nodded. She'd always been

absolutely honest with the woman who had brought her up as her own daughter.

'Yes, I guess he has.'

'Don't you think that's a bit chancy? You don't know anything about him – nobody does. He could be an outlaw–'

'Just as easily could be a ranch hand or a stagecoach driver, or any of a dozen other things.'

'That's true, but you ought to find out, make sure – not get yourself lost in a hopeless situation that could break your heart.'

'By the end of today I'll know all about him,' Sharon had said, bending her knees slightly so that she might better see her reflection in the small mirror suspended from one of the wagon top's arching bows.

Beth had risen from the trunk upon which she was sitting, and handing Sharon a light shawl to throw over her shoulders, exposed by the low-cut dress, drew back to let the girl pass.

'What about Rufus?' she had asked as Sharon climbed down the steps Noah had improvised at the rear of the vehicle.

Sharon had hesitated, her eyes reaching out over the rolling gray-green country before them. A slight frown puckered her brow.

'Rufus will be all right,' she replied. 'He'll always be all right, no matter what. He's that kind.'

Now, on the seat of the wagon watching Adam Gann making a final check of harness before pulling out, Sharon's thoughts were entirely centered upon the tall, somewhat hard-looking man who had so unaccountably captured her interest.

'Morning. Dress you're wearing sure is mighty pretty.'

So intent was she on observing the movements of Gann that it was several moments before she realized that Rufus Enfield was standing beside the wagon speaking to her. Recovering quickly, she smiled down at him.

'Thank you, Rufus. I got a little tired of wearing Pa's old clothes. Thought I'd change.'

Rufus, as tall as Gann, had square, serious features and quick brown eyes that, constantly moving, missed nothing.

'That the only reason?' he asked pointedly.

Sharon smiled again, stirred indifferently, and made some adjustments in the shawl draping her bare shoulders.

'What other could there be?' she countered lightly.

Rufus shook his head, glanced at Adam, now finished with his inspection and moving up. 'I'm beginning to wonder,' he said, and pivoting on a heel, returned to the Price wagon.

Gann paused, followed the younger man with a puzzled look, and then pulled himself up onto the seat, sat down beside the girl. Taking up the reins, foot on the brake, he turned to the back of the wagon.

'Everybody ready?'

'Reckon they are,' Noah McLeod's voice replied. 'Getting late. Let's start moving.'

For answer Adam kicked off the brake, shook the lines, and put the team into motion – pulling away from the clearing where they had made camp and heading up a gentle grade that would lead them out onto a broad mesa.

Sharon stole a glance at Gann. There was a pleased expression on his flat-planed face and in his light, slightly narrowed eyes, as if he enjoyed what he was doing. The thought occurred to her that here, perhaps, was his calling – a stagecoach driver, as she'd suggested to Beth, or a freighter, a teamster of some sort.

'Have you done a lot of driving?' she asked, hoping to start a conversation. So far he had seemingly been unaware of her presence.

'Done my share,' he said.

Sharon frowned. 'I mean, is driving what you do for a living?'

He made no immediate reply, being occupied at that moment in guiding the team up the slope onto the flat. Only when they had crested the rise and gained the level and the rest of the wagons were strung out behind them did he answer.

'Nope, just done a bit of it now and then. I'm a plain, everyday cowhand.'

She smiled. 'I see. Is the ranch where you work somewhere around here?'

'No. Last place was up in Montana. Before that it was here in Arizona, and ahead of that I think it was a spread over in Texas. I'm not much of a hand to stay put anywhere for long.'

'A drifter.' The word, tinged with scorn, escaped Sharon's lips before she thought.

She felt his glance upon her, pressing, curious, and assessing.

'You don't like a man following that kind of a life?' he asked, amusement in his tone.

Her shoulders stirred. 'Never gave it much thought, but most men like to settle down, have a home, a wife and family – build something for themselves.'

'Could be doing the same someday.'

'Are you married?'

'Nope. Been too busy seeing the country, I reckon, or maybe I just haven't come across the right woman.'

His voice broke off abruptly and he fell silent as if he had said something he instantly regretted – or that it was a subject he would as soon avoid. Sharon slid another side look at him, saw that he was staring straight ahead, his features strong, almost chiseled in the growing sunlight.

There was something dark in his mind,

intuition told her – something hidden that she was not privileged to share. But it had nothing to do with another woman, or a wife, and that was a relief.

'It's going to be a fine day,' she said. 'I think I shall enjoy it.'

He turned to her then, his eyes taking in her face, her softly coiled hair, the smooth lines of her neck, the push of her breasts against the front of her dress.

'Goes for me, too,' he said with a smile, and slapping the lagging horses with the slack in the lines, urged them to a faster pace.

Chapter 11

'Sounds like a war,' John Olson said. 'What do you figure's going on down there?'

Noah McLeod, elbows resting on his knees as he leaned forward, thick, stubby hands wrapped about the leathers, glanced at Gann for an answer. It was the third day since Adam had taken charge, and the members of the train now looked to him for an explanation for anything that arose pertaining to the country, and accepted his advice, usually, in other matters.

'It's a place called Dragoon Pass,' he said. 'Was there a couple of years ago. Cowtown – and a pretty wild one. We'd be smart to pass it up.'

'Pass it up!' Olson echoed in dismay. 'Hell, I can't do that. We're running short on grub – plumb out of some things. My old woman says if we don't do some stocking up, we ain't going to eat.'

'Goes for me, too,' Daniel Price said. 'And from what I hear tell, rest of the folks are in the same shape.'

McLeod shifted on the seat of the wagon. 'Maybe we can get by, if it's needful. How far to the next town, Adam?'

'Three, maybe four days.'

'Too far,' Jim Ritter said flatly. 'Can't hold out that long. What's wrong with us going in and doing some trading in this Dragoon Pass, or whatever it's called?'

Rufus Enfield, arms folded across his chest, hostility in his manner, said: 'That's something I'd like to know. There a reason why you don't want to be seen there, Gann?'

Adam's jaw tightened slightly at Enfield's tone, and then, taking no offense, he passed it off. Rufus hadn't been the same toward him since that day he'd driven for Noah and Sharon had ridden the entire time on the seat beside him. They had enjoyed each other, talking about everything that had come to mind.

But he reckoned a man with his sights set on marrying a woman could be expected to get a bit jealous when she got all dolled up and spent the day in another man's company. Rufus didn't have the right to feel that way, however, according to the things Sharon had said. He had no claim on her – she had made that clear; he might think so, but he was wrong.

At that point Adam had also made something clear – that he had no plans for the future insofar as settling down was concerned. He wasn't certain, though, that the girl had accepted the declaration, mainly because she had tried to exact specific reasons from him as to why, and he couldn't find it in his heart to tell her that he was a convicted killer who had escaped from the law, was on the run, and therefore could look forward to nothing.

'Nope, neither here nor there to me,' he replied, and stared off in the direction of the settlement. The rapping of guns was steady, like a string of firecrackers going off on Independence Day. 'Any of you know what happens when a town gets treed?'

Ritter and the others, gathered at the side of the McLeod wagon after Gann, riding with him, had called a halt, glanced back and forth. Enfield shrugged as if not interested and shifted his attention to the rear of the vehicle where Sharon had appeared.

'Don't reckon none of us has,' Noah said. 'That what all the shooting's about?'

'That'd be my guess,' Gann said. 'That's what folks call it when a bunch of cowhands ride into a town and start shooting up the place. Sometimes they're just busting loose, celebrating; other times they've got it in for the town for some reason.'

'Like what?' Ritter asked, finding it difficult to understand.

'Well, maybe they think the merchants cheated them, or it could be the town's lawman got a bit rough with one of their bunch, or they figure he's too strict.

'There's plenty of reasons, and they don't

need but one little one when there's a bunch of them all liquored up. You've got to remember that men like them don't get into a town very often – sometimes it's months – and they're sort of boiling over and aching to blow off steam. Anybody that crosses them or gets in their way or tries to stop them usually winds up with the worst end of the deal.'

'All that shooting – are they trying to kill somebody?'

Adam shook his head. 'Probably not. Most of them are aiming at the sky, and pulling the trigger just to make a noise. Of course, there's some that target-practice on the signs and windows along the street – even the bell in a church steeple if there's one around.'

'Then it ain't nothing but a lot of crazy tomfoolery.'

'Could say that, but folks get hurt, sometimes killed, by a stray bullet, or run over by a horse.'

'I expect we can take care of ourselves when it comes to a bunch like that,' John Olson said. 'We managed to during the war when we had Yankees and deserters running loose all over our property, and then afterwards when–'

'For certain,' Daniel Price cut in. 'And we've got guns – leastwise rifles and shotguns. Charley's the only man with a pistol.'

Gann shook his head. 'You'll be better off

unarmed if you're going in.'

'Not me!' Rufus declared, coming back around. 'I'll be carrying my rifle.'

'Same here,' Olson said. 'It don't make sense walking into a bunch like that without a weapon of some kind.'

Adam rubbed at his jaw, glanced at Sharon as if hoping she was beyond earshot, and then faced the men.

'You won't be liking this much,' he said, 'but you'd best hear it. You folks are what cattle people and cowhands call "hay-shakers" or "sodbuster" or "corncrackers", and there's hardly anybody or anything they hate worse.'

'We've been called names like that before,' Jim Ritter said.

'Maybe, but not by men like you'll run into down there. They figure your kind is the ruination of the country, that you're killing the cattle business by plowing up the land and building fences and roads and such, and they're set on driving you out.'

'We're passing through, not settling here,' McLeod pointed out. 'Ought to make a difference was we to tell them that.'

'*If* you can get the chance, and you might if you'll go in without any weapons showing. Do it that way and likely all that'll happen is you'll get shoved around a bit. Might be some of them'll unload a few bullets at your feet to make you dance, or you could get roped and dragged along the street–'

'They sure as hell better not try that on me!' Charley Ritter stated, patting the holstered pistol on his hip. 'I'll–'

'Forget it,' Adam said. 'You wouldn't live long enough to draw it. Oh, sure, I know you can use a gun. But you'd better remember that those men down there live with one – and they're never without it. They don't just shoot once in a while, maybe at a hawk or a rabbit, like you do. They're using their six-guns regularly every day, practicing, you could say. And they're not only quick at drawing one, but most of them are dead shots.'

Silence followed Gann's admonition, the hush broken only by the fretful crying of Jim Ritter's young son back in the wagon, and the sharp, challenging bark of a gopher watching the meeting from a few yards away.

'So what you're saying is that if we go into that town, we'd best go without our guns, that it?' McLeod said, boiling it all down into few words.

Adam nodded. 'If you're set on going in, that's my advice. You'll probably get kicked around some because you're farmers, but you'll come back with a whole skin.'

Charley Ritter cocked his head to one side, considered Gann narrowly. 'How about you? You be armed?'

Gann said, 'Will if I can borrow a rifle

from somebody.'

Rufus Enfield laughed. 'Guess that means all you been saying don't apply to you.'

'Means I know how to handle myself in a bunch like that, and I don't figure you do,' Gann responded coldly.

'Well, I vote we go in,' Olson said, and smiled up at Adam. 'We all appreciate your advice, Gann, and I expect we'd be heeding it just like we have been 'cepting we don't have no choice this time. We're all needing grub. Was only us menfolk we could probably do what you ask and keep moving till we come to the next town, but we've got our women to think of, and the little ones.'

'Way I feel, too,' Daniel Price said. 'And them that wants to carry a gun, let them. I'm listening to Adam because I figure he knows what he's talking about, and leaving mine in the wagon. All I aim to do is slip in there, buy what I'm needing, and slip back out.'

'I agree,' Olson said. 'Exactly what I'm doing.'

'And me,' Jim Ritter echoed.

Charley Ritter nodded to his brother. 'Well, I'll be going too, but I sure don't aim to go without my pistol–'

'Count me in with you,' Rufus interrupted. 'I'll be toting my gun, no matter what anybody says.'

Adam smiled, shrugged indifferently. 'Up to you,' he said, and turned to McLeod.

'Can't quite recollect the lay of the town, but I think there's a grove of trees at this end. Be smart to pull in there, leave the wagons and the women. Not apt to be bothered if they ain't seen.'

'Just what we'll do,' McLeod said, and swept the men still grouped nearby with his glance. 'You hear Gann? We'll be pulling up in the trees this side of the town. Let's get down there and get this over with.'

Chapter 12

'I ain't so sure about this now,' Noah McLeod said as he drew his wagon to a halt in the trees at the edge of the town. 'That bunch is mighty wild.'

Adam, on the seat beside the Virginian, let his gaze run along Dragoon Pass's only street. Of brief length, and wide, it was a canyon of trapped dust, powder smoke, and noise as half a dozen or so raiders raced back and forth firing their pistols. Other cowhands, on foot, were wandering along the board sidewalks, recklessly shooting at whatever took their fancy – signs, hitching posts, windows, chimney pipes. Over near one of the saloons a dog lay dead by a water trough, victim of the senseless vandalism harassing the settlement.

'Be a good idea if you'd pass it up,' Gann said. 'That bunch is sure fired up.'

'I see now what you was trying to tell us,' McLeod replied. 'Didn't figure it'd be this bad.'

'We're going on in.' Charley Ritter's voice came to them, bringing their attention about.

Ritter, astride one of the spare horses,

Rufus Enfield on the other, trotted by, heading for the end of the street.

'Wait!' McLeod shouted after them. 'Best we all go in together. Be safer–'

But the two men, either unhearing or un-heeding, continued on their way. Noah turned to Adam, started to speak. He checked his words as Price, John Olson, and Jim Ritter halted at the front wheel of his wagon.

'You coming?' Olson asked.

'Reckon I am,' McLeod replied reluct-antly, and twisting about on the seat, called: 'Beth, you got that there list of what you're needing ready?'

He didn't wait for a response. Grasping the curved iron handle of the seat, he climbed down from the wagon. As Gann followed, both Sharon and Beth came from the rear of the vehicle, the latter with a fold of paper in her hand which she passed to Noah.

'Be careful,' she cautioned. 'We can make out without the groceries we're needing, but I can't do without you.'

'Don't fret none over it,' Noah said. 'I sure don't aim to be no hero.'

'All right if I borrow your rifle?' Adam asked, reaching under the seat of the wagon for the weapon.

'Help yourself,' McLeod replied and glanced at the others. 'Are you all still agreed this is something we've got to do?'

Olson said: 'Ain't no choice, Noah.'

McLeod nodded, shrugged. 'Anybody else carrying a gun?'

'None of us,' Ritter said. 'We're taking Gann's advice. Sure wish't I could've made Charley do the same, but he insisted on wearing that damned pistol.'

'Had the same trouble with Rufus,' Daniel Price said. 'Told him he'd be better off leaving that scatter-gun of his in the wagon. Wouldn't listen.'

'I'm a mite worried about Charley,' Jim Ritter said, his eyes following his brother and Enfield, now entering the street. 'Expect I'd better go on ahead.'

'We'll all go,' McLeod said, watching Adam lever the rifle as he checked the chamber for a load. 'The magazine's full.'

Gann closed the action of the weapon, hung it in the crook of an arm, and shifted his attention to Sharon and Beth.

'You ladies stay inside the wagons. Be obliged if you'll pass the word on to the others,' he said, and with a nod to the girl, fell in beside McLeod and the others, moving off toward town.

'We best get our buying done quick and get out of here,' Noah said, his gaze on the noisy confusion swirling along the street. 'No place for us – no place for any sane man – and the sooner we're gone the better I'll feel about it.'

'There's my horse,' Jim Ritter said as they drew nearer to the twin rows of buildings. 'Over there – in front of that saloon. Charley and Rufus must've gone inside for a drink.'

Adam swore. The two men were really pushing their luck. A saloon filled with drunken cowhands was the last place a couple of sodbusters should go. He grinned tautly, realizing he was applying the same derogatory term to the men of the wagon train that cattlemen would use. It had been without conscious thought; a cowhand himself and always having worked around such, it had come naturally.

'Where's the general store?' Olson wondered. 'Anybody spot it? Damn dust and smoke's so thick I–'

'Find it on your left – about halfway down the street,' Gann answered. 'Keep on the sidewalks all you can. Good chance of getting run over out here.'

Two riders raced up, yelling, one swinging a rope.

They saw the tight group of men, jerked their horses to a sliding stop.

'Now, what've we got here?' one shouted.

Gann changed the rifle from the crook of his arm to a ready position in both hands.

'Trouble – if that's what you're looking for,' he said coolly, and then added at low breath to McLeod and the others, 'Keep moving.'

'Trouble!' the man with the rope echoed thickly. 'You won't ever see the day when a lousy squat–'

Gann whipped the rifle about, triggered a shot. Dust spurted up at the feet of the rider's horse, sending the animal shying and hopping nervously. Adam slid a glance at McLeod and the men with him; they had gained the broad sidewalk, were hurrying toward the general store.

'As soon blow your head off with my next bullet,' he said, coming back to the cow-hand.

The rider had managed to settle down his horse. He stared at Gann for a long breath as he drew in his rope.

'Yeh, reckon you would,' he said, and jamming spurs to his mount, spun about and rushed off down the street. His partner, also considering Adam with a sort of respectful suspicion, followed.

Gann looked again to the store. McLeod, with Price and Olson beside him, were entering the doorway. Jim Ritter had paused on the landing, eyes on the saloon into which his brother and Rufus Enfield had gone. After a few moments he pivoted, followed the other men into the store.

Elsewhere along the street, horses were pounding back and forth, and while the shooting had dropped off somewhat, there was no slackening of activity. Across from the low-roofed structure bearing a bullet-pocked sign that designated it as a hotel, two riders had their loops about a hitchrack, had yanked it out of the sun-baked ground and were heading for the far end of town, dragging it behind them.

Another cowhand, wearing a high-crowned black hat, had managed to get on the porch roof of the building next to the saloon and was standing upright, swaying uncertainly while he emptied his pistol at the metal weathervane topping a nearby structure. Abruptly, a riderless horse appeared in the haze. Galloping madly, it veered sharply to avoid colliding with another horse, and then swerved into the passageway lying between the saloon and its neighbor, and disappeared.

Gann, the rifle again slung from the crook of his left arm and wishing the pilgrims would get their business over with so that they might leave before any serious problems developed, threw a glance over a shoulder at the wagons. He could see Sharon and Beth on the seat of McLeod's. Standing nearby, at the edge of the trees, were two other women, but at that distance he was unable to tell who they were. All, no doubt, were watching and waiting anxiously.

He'd best do what he could to hurry things up, Adam decided. He hadn't thought the wagons would be so visible from the town, and wondered if the women hadn't moved them a bit in order to better see what was taking place along the street. It had been a dangerous thing to do, if true; some of the cowhands, spotting them, could take it in mind to ride out and have themselves some fun.

Angling toward the walk, avoiding a race in progress between two cowboys, Adam struck out for the general store. McLeod and the others were not in sight, so therefore must still be inside making their purchases. They were lucky the merchant was still open for business. Most times, under such trying circumstances, he would have locked his doors in hopes of avoiding as much damage as possible. It could be that–

Gann drew to a halt. The swinging doors of the saloon had burst open. Two men, gripping each other, swaying back and forth, plunged into view. They seemed to hesitate for a long breath and then both fell full length into the dust as a dozen onlookers, all yelling and cheering, streamed out in their wake. The two on the ground, kicking and thrashing, broke apart and came to their feet and began to trade blows.

Adam swore in frustration, and changing course, hurried toward the crowd gathering around the pair. One of them was Rufus Enfield.

Chapter 13

As Gann pivoted and cut back across the street for the saloon at a fast walk, others along the way were wheeling, abandoning whatever they were doing, and hastening toward the new attraction.

Adam reached the crowd, all shouting encouragement to their man – a squat redhead with thick blacksmith arms and a broad, flat face. Rufus, nose bloodied, lips crushed, dust covering his clothing, was holding his own, however, against the cowboy, who appeared to be stronger but lacked ability to move quickly.

Gann saw Charley Ritter at that moment. He was standing almost directly opposite in the crowd, and was completely surrounded by cowhands and other saloon hangers-on and a few townsmen who dared to be abroad. Ritter's features were taut as he watched the two fighters circling warily inside the enclosure of bystanders.

'Come on, Red – get him!' a voice shouted imploringly.

'You can't let no stinking hayshaker get the best of you!'

'Use your head!'

As if hearing, Red paused. Suddenly ducking low, he rushed Enfield. Rufus endeavored to jump aside, avoid the charge. He came up against several of Red's friends. They reached out, blocked his movements, sent him stumbling forward to collide solidly with his opponent.

Breath gushed from Enfield's mouth in a windy blast as Red's head drove into his middle. He sank to his knees, sucking deeply. Hands reached down, dragged him upright, held him rigid.

'Here he is, Red! He's all yours!' someone shouted. A chorus of cheers sounded.

The stocky cowhand grinned, moved in. Hamlike fists cocked, he started a blow for Enfield's jaw. Immediately, Adam Gann shouldered his way into the circle, roughly pushing bystanders aside until he had reached the sagging Rufus. Swinging his rifle in a quick arc, he blocked the redhead's blow.

A fresh burst of yells lifted, angry at the interference. Adam ignored them, raised a hand, and placing his palm in the face of the man pinning Enfield's arms to his sides, shoved him away.

'Keep out of it!' he snarled. 'This is one to one!'

The cowboy reeled back, tripped, fell. The man who had been standing beside him, face flushed from liquor, eyes snapping, surged forward.

'Who the hell do you think you are?' he demanded.

'I'm the man who told him – and you – to back off!' Gann snapped, and with a quick flip of his rifle, slapped the stock hard against the cowpuncher's jaw, dropping him without a sound into the ankle-deep dust.

'Goes for everybody!' Gann shouted, making himself heard above the hubbub. 'Let them settle it on their own!'

He became aware then that attention had shifted from Rufus and the redhead, again sparring warily as each sought an opening for a telling blow, to the front of the saloon. The crowd was separating, dividing, backing away, getting clear of two men, half crouched and facing one another through the thin layers of drifting tan haze.

Charley Ritter! Recognition came to Adam in that next breath. Charley was squaring off with a lean, light-haired man – intending to shoot it out! Alarm rocked through him. Ritter didn't have a chance. Pushing forward, he started for the two men. If he could get there in time he could step in between, stop the shooting before it could take place. He was ten seconds too late.

The blond buckled forward. His gun came up, fired, a coil of smoke belching from its muzzle. Ritter staggered back, a look of surprise on his face. His weapon was only half out of its holster.

Adam, working his way through the abruptly quiet crowd, reached Ritter as he went down. Kneeling beside him he saw at once that Charley was dead – killed instantly by the heavy-caliber bullet that had ripped into his chest.

There was a commotion in the gathering. Adam drew himself upright, looked around. It was Jim Ritter. The big homesteader halted, eyes on the still figure of his brother.

'Knew this was going to happen,' Ritter said in a hard, controlled voice, and raised his narrowed eyes to the crowd. 'Who done it?'

Gann looked more closely at Ritter. Usually calm and quiet, the man was now like a powder keg ready to explode.

'Let it go, Jim,' he said quietly. 'It's over. It don't matter who–'

'Don't matter!' Ritter echoed bitterly. 'Charley was my brother, and I sure ain't letting no–'

'Was a fair fight,' a man in the front of the gathering said, shaking his head. 'We all seen it. Your brother was spoiling for trouble. Called Pete a hard name. Ended up with them going for their guns.'

'Was nothing fair about it!' Ritter snapped. 'Charley wasn't no gunman.'

'Then he sure was a damn fool to call Pete Meeker out! He's one of the best.'

'Makes no difference – I ain't letting the killing pass,' Ritter shot back in the same bitter tone.

'That mean you're looking for trouble, too, sodbuster?' a voice asked. The crowd parted, allowing the slim, blond gunslinger to step into the clear and face Jim Ritter. 'I'm Peter Meeker and I'll be real pleased to accommodate you, same as I did your brother. Just you get yourself a gun–'

'No!'

Jim Ritter's yell was high, unnatural. He lunged forward, rage and grief overcoming him. His big hands shot out, caught Meeker by the throat and belt buckle. Pivoting, he lifted the man off his feet, slammed him to the ground.

Instantly, a shout went up and the crowd surged toward the homesteader. Gann stepped quickly in beside him. Grim, he fired a shot into the ground at the feet of the nearest men. They hesitated. Tight-lipped, Adam waved them back with the muzzle of his weapon.

'One dead man's enough!' he grated. 'Don't give me a reason to make it two – or more!'

A tense hush followed his brittle words, one broken only by the dry, scuffing sound of boots against the sandy soil as the men realigned themselves. One of the cowhands in the front, young, curly hair down to his shoulders, skin glistening from the heat, spat, shook his head.

'There ain't but one of you,' he said, 'and you sure can't shoot us all.'

Adam smiled thinly. 'Reckon not,' he drawled. 'But I'll get a few – and you'll be the first one. Now, back off. This ruckus is ending right here.'

On beyond the crowd he could see Rufus Enfield, standing dust-caked and sweat-soaked, his fight with Red either concluded or abandoned. Farther over were Olson, McLeod, and Daniel Price, sacks containing their purchases thrown over their shoulders.

'We're leaving!' Gann continued, his voice loud and clear. 'Any man that tries stopping us will get the worst of it. Rufus – bring the horses over here!'

Enfield turned at once for the saloon's hitchrack. Adam, lowering himself by bending his knees so that his eyes might remain on the glowering cowhands, picked up Charley Ritter's pistol and thrust it under his belt.

'Help Rufus,' he said to Jim as Enfield approached, leading the two mounts. The homesteader seemed dazed, almost unaware of what was going on.

The crowd broke apart, reluctantly, permitted Rufus to move in close and halt. Together Enfield and Jim Ritter lifted the lifeless body and laid it across the saddle of one of the horses, doing so under the watchful eye and ready rifle of Gann.

'Keep going,' Adam directed, clearing a path for the two men and the horses with the threatening muzzle of his weapon.

Rufus, leading his mount, Jim Ritter with the one bearing Charley, moved off into the street toward McLeod and the others, waiting a few strides away.

'The hell with him!' the redhead who had fought with Rufus shouted, coming out of the crowd as Adam stepped in to cover the retreat of Ritter and Enfield. 'We going to let a bunch of clodhoppers buffalo us?'

'No!' the answer went up from half a dozen throats. 'Let's get 'em!'

Gann, walking backward slowly, halted. He heard Ritter and Rufus bang the horses to a stop.

'Go on,' he said in a low voice. 'I can handle this.'

The crowd had paused also, now stood facing him in the haze of dust filling the street. Meeker was in the forefront, he saw, along with the redhead, who looked as if he'd gotten the worst of the encounter with Enfield, and the curly-haired cowhand. Adam, his rifle up, hammer cocked, considered them for a long breath.

'Curly, you decided you want to die first?' he asked, finally, centering his attention on the cowhand. 'Standing out there in front like that sort of gives me the idea.'

From the tail of an eye Gann could see that Rufus and Jim Ritter had joined McLeod and the others, and all were moving hurriedly for the wagons. He became aware of the muttering crowd, and turned his attention to Pete Meeker. The gunman, arms hanging loosely at his sides, fingers splayed, was staring at him with steady intent. Again, Gann's mouth split into a tight smile.

'What's on your mind, Pete? You want to make it just me and you, shooting it out?'

Meeker gave no reply, simply continued to stare.

'It'll be fine with me,' Adam went on in a conversational tone, 'but I best warn you ahead of time though – I'll kill you. I ain't no sodbuster like that man you shot down. Think it over.'

A flicker of uncertainty crossed Meeker's narrow features. Nearby, Red shifted nervously, hawked, spat into the loose dust. Gann glanced at Curly, whose attention had also strayed to elsewhere along the street. Then, the same hard smile persisting, he resumed his slow, backward march.

'Giving you some good advice – all of you; turn around and go get yourself a drink. Try following me and it'll be the last thing you ever do.'

There was only silence for several

moments, and then someone said: 'Aw, what the hell!' Immediately, the crowd began to break up, drift back toward the saloon. All but Pete Meeker. He continued to stand motionless in the streaming sunshine, shoulders sloped, head dropped forward as he watched Adam's retreat.

Gann, never taking his eyes off the gunman, continued his deliberate pace along the center of the street. Pete might take a sudden notion to make a move and he didn't intend to be caught unawares. But the thinfaced killer seemed disinclined to press the point, and finally reaching what he considered a safe distance beyond pistol range, Adam wheeled, and brushing away the sweat beading his forehead, hurried on to the wagons.

Chapter 14

Noah McLeod and the others were gathered at the Ritter wagon. They had taken Charley's body off his horse, laid it in the back of the vehicle, and were expressing their condolences to Jim and his wife. As Gann came up, they turned, greeted him quietly.

McLeod extended his hand. 'Sure grateful to you for what you done.'

'Took a brave man to stand up against that bunch of drunks,' Price added.

Gann shook his head. Just beyond Noah McLeod he could see Sharon. She was looking directly at him, her eyes glowing, a proud smile on her lips.

'Part of what you hired me to do,' he said, looking away.

'Maybe,' Olson said, 'but taking on a whole bunch like that–'

'There's a lot in knowing how to handle their kind,' Gann cut in. 'Not sure it's going to stick, however.'

McLeod frowned. 'What do you mean by that?'

'Can't see that gunman, Meeker, letting it drop. Soon as he and some of his pals belt down a few drinks, I figure they'll come looking to finish what they tried to start.'

'So, what'd we best do?'

'Pull out – right away.'

McLeod nodded slowly, turned his attention to Jim Ritter. 'It all right with you if we hold up burying Charley until we're a piece from here?'

Ritter shrugged indifferently. 'Here or there's not going to matter to him – or me,' he said, and reaching into the wagon, picked up the cartridge belt and holster his brother had been wearing and handed it to Adam. 'You might as well have this – goes with that pistol.'

Gann smiled and said, 'Obliged to you,' and strapping the holster about his waist, took the pistol from his belt, dropped it into the oil-slick leather. It felt good to be wearing iron again, but he made no mention of that, knowing the homesteaders would not understand.

'Like to ask a favor of you now,' he said, still facing Ritter. 'Need to borrow one of your horses. One your brother was riding will do fine.'

'Help yourself,' Ritter said woodenly. Then, 'You going somewhere?'

'No, aim to hang back and keep an eye on the road after you all have pulled out. If Meeker and his friends show up, I want to be waiting for them.'

Abruptly, Gann wheeled, crossed to where

Charley Ritter's mount was standing, and swung up onto the saddle. Cutting about, he paused in front of McLeod.

'Keep heading north. I'll catch up by dark.'

He felt Sharon's gaze upon him, gave her a brief nod, and then caught the steady pressure of Rufus Enfield's eyes, doubting, suspicious. Evidently Rufus thought he was pulling out, leaving the wagon train flat.

'I'll be back,' he said, and pulling away from the party, already preparing to move on, rode to the end of the grove where he could best see the settlement.

There was no activity in front of the saloon, and the street was now quiet, devoid of riders as well as pedestrians, leaving only thin clouds of drifting dust and the wreckage as witness to what had transpired only minutes earlier. It was a bad sign, Gann thought, leaning back in the saddle.

If the cowhands had resumed their hoorawing the town, he would be inclined to believe they had forgotten the incident with the pilgrims and Pete Meeker had decided he'd suffered no loss of face after all. Instead, however, they were all apparently still inside the saloon where they could be hashing things over while Meeker nursed his pride, and with his closer friends, fortified his courage with strong liquor.

Twisting about, Adam threw a glance over

his shoulder. The wagons were moving on. He had turned just in time to catch a glimpse of the last vehicle in the train, Olson's, disappearing into the trees. He felt a stir of relief. That was good. If Meeker and the cowhands continued to salve their wounds with whiskey for another hour or so, the McLeod party would be well on its way.

Little more than half of that time had elapsed when Adam Gann drew himself to attention. The riders were coming out of the saloon. He watched them straggle into the street, circle the building, and reappear shortly on their horses. A discourse of some sort ensued for several minutes, and then four of them broke away from the rest and pointed for the grove.

Gann considered them narrowly, endeavoring to establish their identities. Pete Meeker for sure, Curly, the redhead, and a fourth man he'd not noticed before. Slack in the saddle, Adam allowed the men to draw close. When they had reached what he felt was a deadline, he abruptly rode out and confronted them.

'Can you see you don't believe in warnings!' he said coldly, letting his hand rest on the pistol at his side.

The riders had come to a sudden stop. Curly swore, and the fourth man, somewhat flushed from liquor, raised his hands quickly.

'I ain't got no quarrel with you, mister!'

'Then get the hell out of here!' Gann snapped. 'Your friends there think they have – and they're about to meet up with it!'

Curly, lifting his arms cautiously, shook his head. 'Count me out, too. This ain't none of my doing.'

Adam fixed his cold gaze on Red. 'How about you? Where you standing in this? You wanting to die alongside Pete there?'

'Could be you that'll be dying,' Meeker said, and made a stab for his gun.

Gann drew and fired in a quick blur of motion. The two shots blended almost into one. Adam felt the tug of Meeker's bullet as it tore through the cloth of his shirt below his left arm, but he gave it no thought. His attention was on the men with Meeker, on the gunman, alert for any indication that they were going to take a hand, or that Meeker would try a second time.

But Pete was doubling forward on his saddle in a slow, weary way, and Curly and the two men with him were sitting rigidly on their horses, arms well away from their sides to show they had no intention of taking up the shootout.

Tension draining from him, Gann watched, his pistol still in his hand and leveled at the men. Abruptly, Pete Meeker tumbled to the ground, sprawling full length. Only then did Adam's concentration break. He drew himself back on the saddle, nodded briskly to Meeker's friends.

'Load him up and take him back to town,' he said. 'And don't try following me. Told you that before.'

Both Curly and Red came off their horses, and making no comment, lifted Meeker's body and hung it over his saddle. The fourth man kneed his mount in close, took the reins.

'I make myself clear?' Gann pressed softly.

Curly, back on his horse, nodded. 'I reckon you have,' he said, and with Red and the fourth man leading Pete Meeker's mount, swung about and headed back for town.

Adam watched them until they were well on their way, and then wheeling, set out after the wagon train at a brisk lope.

Chapter 15

Charley Ritter was buried at sunset that day, shortly after camp was made. Since there was no lumber available for a coffin, he was first wrapped in a blanket and then in a square of canvas before being lowered into his grave.

Noah McLeod quoted appropriate words from his worn, leather-backed bible after which each of the men spoke kindly of Charley. By the time the light had failed the simple service was over and the headstone prepared by John Olson was in place.

There followed a quiet, subdued evening with no one feeling much like gathering around the fire to talk, as was the usual custom, and soon after supper was over all but Adam had retired.

The day's events had left him restless and disturbed, and when the last of the wagon train people had taken their leave, he stamped out the fire and, rifle in hand, dropped back along the road for a quarter mile or so. There, on a slight rise that afforded him a fine view of the country spreading out before him, he settled down.

He didn't believe there would be any further trouble from Pete Meeker's friends or the cowhands they had encountered at Dragoon Pass, but since sleep seemed far from him, he figured he might as well keep an eye on the road for a while. Gann had scarcely made himself comfortable in the low brush, shoulders against a boulder, when the faint scuff of someone approaching from the camp drew his attention. Leaning forward, he strained to see who it was.

A moment later he drew back. It was Sharon McLeod. She had halted in the center of the road, was glancing about endeavoring to locate him. Wearing a robe of some sort over her night clothing, dark hair hanging about her shoulders, she looked unreal, a pale apparition in the starlight.

'Adam,' she called softly.

Gann made no reply. He would have liked nothing better than to give way to his feeling, become closer to Sharon, and build something strong and magical between them, but it wouldn't be fair to her. There simply was no future in it – not for either of them. He had only a slim chance of beating the law by slipping into Mexico, and he'd not drag her into a situation where the odds were all stacked against their making a life together.

It was a decision he'd made earlier, shortly after they had met, and now as the days and nights passed during which they found themselves in each other's company almost continually, Gann was finding it more and more difficult to stand by that determination.

Sharon called out once more, softly, as if she feared to draw the attention of someone in camp, and then when he did not answer, she turned, made her way back to the wagons.

That next morning as they ate an early meal, Adam felt her eyes upon him several times, curious, wondering, and he was pressed to not reveal in some way that he had intentionally avoided her. Such resulted in a polite reserve springing up between them, and for the ensuing days as they continued steadily on a due-north course, conversation between them was but occasional.

Fortunately, a change in duties since the incident at Dragoon Pass now called for him to serve as outrider for the train, and as such he was in the saddle, using alternately one and then the other of Jim Ritter's spare horses as he ranged ahead, seeking the best trail to follow, the few available water sources, and the more suitable places to pitch camp.

Adam assumed his new responsibilities, proposed by Daniel Price and immediately endorsed by the others, with a mixture of relief and gratitude. For one thing, he was at home on a horse; as it was with all cowhands, walking or riding in a wagon was a chore not to his liking. Too, he was removed from Sharon McLeod and the hunger for her that he struggled to suppress.

Several times he wished they would come to a town where the girl and Rufus Enfield could be married, if that was the way it was to be. Such would end it for him, put a stop to his yearning, once and for all time.

That possibility prompted him to advise Noah and the other men the evening of the fourth night out of Dragoon Pass that they were approaching a settlement of some size.

'Prescott, the place is called. Capital of the territory. We could lay over there a day or two, if you like, rest the horses, build up your supplies.'

'Nothing I'm needing,' McLeod said, glancing around the circle of men and women ringing the fire. Supper was finished and it was the time for relaxing and drinking chicory coffee while hashing over the day's incidents and experiences. 'How about the rest of you all? You got any trading to do? Gann says we're coming to a good town.'

Olson shook his head. 'Got all we was wanting at that last place.'

'Same here,' Price said, and turned his attention to Jim Ritter, dangling his young son on a knee. 'How about it, you running short on anything?'

'Nope, nothing,' Ritter replied in a flat voice. He had not been the same since his brother's death, the tragedy seemingly having drained off much of his enthusiasm for a new life in a new land.

Despite the fact that he had mentioned the possibility of visiting the settlement as a means for solving one personal problem, Gann was relieved at the parties' rejection of the idea. It would be risky for him to be seen in a town such as Prescott. By that time, lawmen throughout the country would have been advised of his escape, and a new charge – a natural assumption – that of murdering his captor, Deputy Marshal Frank Slawson, would have been added to his crimes. Wanted posters displaying his likeness would be in evidence everywhere.

'I'd like going by so's I can buy myself a gun,' Rufus Enfield said.

The incident at Dragoon Pass had brought about a change in him, also, sobering and aging him somewhat.

'Gun?' Price echoed. 'You got one.'

'Ain't got a pistol, and that's what I'm talking about,' Rufus said. 'A man's got to wear one out here if he's going to be somebody.'

Adam glanced at Sharon, wondering what effect Enfield's words would have on her. She was sitting beside Beth McLeod, leaning forward, elbows on her knees, face soft-edged and lovely as she stared into the fire. If she heard or cared what Rufus had said, she gave no indication.

Gann looked away quickly, the far-reaching loneliness that filled him stirred by the sight of her. She appeared so quiet, so at ease, as the reflection of the flickering tongues of flame danced against her hair, lighted her eyes, and threw moving shadows across her features.

'Well, I reckon we could do it if it's all that important to you, boy,' McLeod said, and nodded to Adam. 'It be much out of the way?'

'Couple of days, more or less.'

Noah gave that thought. 'If we spent a little time there, it'd mean losing maybe a week. I reckon we'd best vote on it.'

'I'm voting no,' Daniel Price stated promptly.

Rufus smiled wryly at his brother-in-law. 'I might've figured you'd be against it just because it's me that's wanting it.'

'You ain't got no business carrying a handgun.'

'Why not? And who're you to be saying that? You still treat me like I was a kid. Damn it to hell, Daniel, I'm growed up now!'

'Watch your language, boy,' McLeod cautioned, frowning darkly. 'There's ladies and young ones here.'

Enfield shrugged helplessly, turned to Ritter. 'Jim, will you loan me a horse? I'll ride up to this here town by myself and get me a pistol.'

Ritter was wagging his head even before Rufus had finished his request. 'Was it for

115

anything but that, I'd say yes. I ain't having nothing to do with a gun – not ever, not as long as I live.'

'Then I'll just take out walking!' Rufus declared. 'I aim to have me a pistol, and that's that!'

Adam pulled back from the circle, got to his feet, and moved off into the darkness. He wanted no part of the discussion, just as he had carefully avoided all of the petty arguments and differences that constant association had given rise to between the members of the train as it wound its way westward.

He was pleased they'd not be stopping at Prescott; he'd not be risking arrest by a lawman there, and also, the marriage of Sharon and Rufus would continue to lie somewhere in the future – which was to his liking as well. Realizing that, Adam frowned. He was finding it impossible to understand himself; he had schemed to get them wedded, yet was relieved to know they would not be.

Halting, Gann looked out over a broad, silvered flat that pushed out from the base of the bluff upon which he was standing. All things were blurred, transfigured in the pale light glowing from the velvet sky. Hushed, peaceful, it was an utterly beautiful world, he thought, one that only a man faced with the probability of spending a large part of his life locked away, could fully appreciate.

What a fine wonderful thing it would be to have a ranch out there, somewhere – a place where he could make the dream that had forever lurked in the back of his mind, come true; a wife – like Sharon – children, plenty of land where he could raise cattle and horses, be a man with firmly planted roots, respected by other men.

He had thought of it often as he drifted back and forth across the restless frontier, but always it had been in a half-hearted, indifferent way as if the dream lacked something that prevented it from materializing. Now he knew what had been wrong; he had not met Sharon McLeod and thus the principal inducement to settle down had not been present.

But such was of no consequence now, he thought resignedly, turning and starting back for the camp.

Their meeting had come too late and he could never let her know how much she could have counted in–

Adam's steps slowed as he drew near the tree-encircled swale in which the train had halted for the night. It was too quiet. Something was wrong – he could feel it, sense it. Abruptly a harsh, unfamiliar voice reached him.

'You folks just set right where you are and don't make no wrong moves. We don't want to hurt nobody, 'specially you pretty ladies.'

Chapter 16

Gann swore deeply. Outlaws – probably busters. They were common in that area, where once there had been considerable mining activity. Drawing his pistol, and keeping well in the brush and shadows of the trees, he moved forward silently. He would need to play it smart; busters usually ran in gangs, sometimes numbering up to a dozen, and he was the McLeod's party only hope, since it sounded as if they had been taken completely by surprise.

Adam halted in the darkness cast by a clump of oak. He could see Olson and his wife clearly, and nearby, Daniel Price. The remainder of the wagon train members were only partly visible. Three of the outlaws were in view, all standing at the edge of the firelight – one with a rifle, two with pistols. There were more – at least two – moving about beyond the glow. One was talking, but his voice was at a natural level and Gann could not distinguish what was being said.

Adam studied the restricted scene, endeavoring to come up with a plan that would enable him to close in and overcome the intruders, but the task appeared impossible. The outlaws had scattered themselves completely around the fire; for one man to try and close in, disarm them without endangering the people of the wagon train with a lot of shooting would–

'Just stand easy, friend,' a voice said from the shadows at his side. 'This here's a six-shooter I'm poking into your backbone.'

Stiffening, Adam stared straight ahead, all the while cursing himself for being careless; he should have known they would be aware of his existence; like as not they had watched the camp from the moment the wagons had pulled to a stop.

'Hey, Luke – I got him!' the voice in the darkness behind him shouted.

'All right, Dade, trot him on in here,' one of the men in the camp, apparently the leader of the gang, replied.

Gann felt a sharp pain as the outlaw jabbed him savagely in the spine with the muzzle of his pistol.

'Get moving,' the voice ordered. 'And so's you won't get no smart ideas, put your hands up over your head.'

In the darkness the outlaw hadn't noticed that he had drawn his pistol, was holding it at his side, Adam realized. His jaw tightened. This would likely be his one and only opportunity.

'You're dealing,' he murmured.

'Yes, sir, I sure am,' Dade agreed, and took

a step nearer.

In that same fragment of time Adam Gann whirled, swinging his pistol, clublike. It connected with the outlaw's head. Dade dropped soundlessly to the ground.

'Dade! What's holding you up.'

Adam bent swiftly, recovered the weapon that had fallen from the outlaw's nerveless fingers. Unbuckling the cartridge belt and holster, he hung it over a shoulder and drew himself upright. Armed now with an extra weapon, he looked again to the camp.

'Dade – damn it – you coming?'

'Coming,' Gann replied, mimicking as best he could the voice of the unconscious outlaw.

He was some better off, he thought, as, tension building within him, he worked his way quietly through the trees and heavy brush. He now had two guns, and that improved the odds considerably; but it would still be no cinch. Whatever move he made must be with care, for besides the danger to the people of the wagon train should a shootout evolve, he need also guard against the outlaws' seizing one or more of the members as a hostage.

If somehow he could get one of the pistols to McLeod or one of the other men the situation would be simplified, but just how he could accomplish that without revealing his own presence he couldn't figure. Gann smiled tightly. No matter how he figured it, it boiled down to one thing – it was squarely up to him, and to him alone.

'Damn it, Dade, what're you doing out there?' It was Luke again, his voice impatient, angry.

Tense, Adam paused. 'I'm right here,' he said, again striving to sound like the outlaw he was replacing while carefully maintaining a screen of brush between himself and the camp.

'Took you long enough. Where's the pilgrim?'

'Back there in the woods a piece. Had to knock him cold,' Gann said, easing slightly to one side so that he might better see the camp. So far no harm had been done to any of the wagon train members. All were sitting in a circle around the fire, just as he had left them only minutes earlier.

'Want you and Spruill, there, to start going through the wagons, see what you can find worth taking,' Luke continued, gesturing at one of the outlaws standing nearby. 'Kansas, you rustle up a couple of blankets and spread them out somewheres so's we'll have something to carry the stuff in.'

'Why don't we just take one of the wagons?' Spruill, a squat, dark man in dirty overalls and undershirt, suggested.

'Because it'd slow us up too damn much – and it'd leave tracks,' Luke explained in a weary voice. He was a bit better dressed than his friends in that he was wearing the pants and vest of a suit, a striped silk shirt and a narrow-brimmed hat.

'Thought you said we'd hang around here till first light, seeing as how there's some mighty pretty female women here to keep us company,' another of the outlaws protested.

'Meant it, too,' Luke assured him, 'but I always say, business before pleasure. I've done picked me out–'

'You'll not touch any of our women!' Noah McLeod shouted, springing to his feet. 'I'll not stand for–'

'Set down, grandpa!' Spruill snapped, waving McLeod back with his weapon. 'Ain't nobody going to get hurt around here – 'cepting you if you don't behave. I'd as soon shoot you and any of them other gents as I would holler sooey, if you get to bothering us.'

'And we sure ain't going to hurt them ladies,' the man who had protested the departure to Luke added. 'That ain't what they're for!'

Adam, crouched low, resumed his slow, quiet progress through the brush. He was attempting to reach a point where he would have all of the outlaws in front of him when he showed himself – or at least the majority of them. It was going to be touch and go.

Luke and his bunch were scattered about

in the camp, and to further complicate the problem, many of the pilgrims were in the line of fire.

'Dade, what in the hell are you doing?' Luke shouted impatiently, and then drew up suspiciously. 'Or maybe you ain't Dade and–'

Gann knew he could delay no longer. Both pistols ready, he stepped abruptly from the shadows into the flare of the replenished fire.

'Everybody stay where you are!' he ordered.

Luke took a half step backward in surprise. A curse exploded from his lips as he reached for his pistol. Gann fired instantly at the first indication of the man's intentions. The bullet struck Luke high in the chest, knocking him writhing to the ground as screams of fright from the women mixed with yells from the outlaws.

From the corner of an eye Adam saw Spruill lunge at Sharon, apparently with the thought of using her for a shield or a hostage. Gann triggered the weapon in his right hand. The outlaw hesitated in mid-stride, fell heavily face down.

Gunsmoke hanging about him, the cool night air filled with echoes of the shots, the crying of Ritter's young son, and the anxious shifting of the horses nearby, Adam advanced farther into the clearing. Cool, he faced the remaining outlaws, each standing transfixed in the flickering firelight, watching him narrowly, fearfully.

'Your move,' Gann invited softly.

For a long breath the three men remained frozen, and then one shook his head, slowly began to raise his arms. His companions immediately followed his example.

At that, as if jarred from their state of shock, McLeod, with Olson, Ritter, and Daniel Price, leaped to their feet. Rushing up to the outlaws, they disarmed and bound them with short lengths of rope and dragged them to one side of the camp.

'You'll find one more back up the road a piece,' Gann said as Olson and Ritter came toward him. 'By a pile of rocks.'

They hurried off, and Adam, holstering both pistols, moved toward the center of the camp where Noah McLeod was piling more wood on the fire. The older man straightened up, greeted him with a smile and a firm handshake.

'We're owing you again,' he said. 'The Lord was sure favoring us the day we met.'

'Works both ways,' Adam replied, glancing at Sharon. She and the other women were in a group standing off to the side, talking excitedly. She turned at that moment, saw that he was looking at her. An expression of gratitude crossed her features, and she seemed about to forsake the women, cross to him. Gann deliberately turned about, put his attention again on McLeod.

'Wasn't expecting to get caught by a bunch of outlaws along there,' Noah said, filling his pipe and lighting it.

'Busters,' Adam said. 'Plenty of them around.'

'Busters? What're they?'

Gann explained the term, in common use in this part of the country. Price, stepping up in time to hear, rubbed at his neck wearily.

'This country's sure out to beat a man one way or another,' he said. 'Something waiting around every bend to lay him by the heels.'

'It's a hard land, all right, but a man can lick it if he keeps his eyes open,' Adam agreed, and handed the belted gun he'd taken off the outlaw to Price. 'Thought you might give this outfit to Rufus – if you're of a mind.'

Price took the bit of gear, studying it thoughtfully. The loops of the belt were filled with cartridges that glinted in the firelight, and the pistol, in its dark treated-leather holster, had worn cedar handles. At that moment Ritter and John Olson returned, the latter shaking his head.

'Couldn't find hide or hair of that jasper,' he said. 'Must've come to and took off in the dark. Don't think there's much use looking for him.'

'Forget him,' Gann said. 'He can't cause us any more trouble – we've got his gun.'

'What'll we do with them we've got tied up?' Price wanted to know. He was still holding the weapon Adam had given him in his hand although Rufus Enfield, having completed the task of dragging the two dead outlaws out into the brush, had joined them.

'Have to take them to the nearest town, turn them over to the law,' Gann said.

McLeod muttered his displeasure. 'Means losing time. Why can't we just turn them loose? Long as we've got their weapons they can't do us no harm.'

'They've got horses around here somewheres close,' Ritter said. 'Best we don't forget that.'

'And there's one of them running loose,' John Olson said. 'Can't forget that either.'

'Important thing is they ain't armed now,' McLeod insisted. 'And, having horses, they can ride to somewheres and get something to eat, so they won't starve. What do you think, Adam?'

'Best thing's still to turn them over to the law,' Gann said, and turned to look at the outlaws hunched at the base of a tree just beyond the fire's glow. Behind him he heard Daniel Price speak.

'Here's that shooting outfit you been wanting.'

Adam glanced over his shoulder. Rufus, a

126

wide smile on his face, was buckling on the belt. 'Obliged to you, Daniel.'

'I figured you were maybe right, that you ought to start going around armed,' Price said. 'Except the rest of us better, too, from here on. Can make use of the guns we took off them outlaws. You look mighty impressive, Rufus. Why don't you go over there and do a bit of strutting in front of your best girl?'

Enfield's grin broadened. He looked at Sharon. Letting his hand rest on the butt of the weapon at his hip, he said, 'Yeh, I think I'll just do that,' and with a pronounced swagger, moved off.

Abruptly he halted. Sharon had stepped away from the other women, who were separating and going to their wagons. Ignoring Rufus, and with a smile on her lips, she was crossing to Adam Gann.

Chapter 17

Sharon stared unseeingly at the road ahead, the reins slack in her hands. She was taking a turn at driving, Noah electing to walk for a spell and stretch his legs. Beth lay in the back of the wagon, a bit under the weather. It was nothing serious, just that she was tired from the long, tedious trip.

It had been two days since the gang of outlaws had attempted to rob the train, and the recollection of Adam standing there in the glow of the fire, a pistol in each hand as he coolly ordered them to surrender, was still a graphic picture in her mind. They had buried the pair he had been forced to kill that same night, and later, sometime in the early morning hours, the three they had captured and intended to turn over to the law in the next town they came to, managed to escape.

It was believed that the man who had gotten away earlier, after being knocked unconscious by Adam, had been able to slip in and free his friends while everyone was asleep, including Rufus, who while taking his turn at standing watch over the outlaws succumbed to weariness, during which time the busters took their leave. They elected, apparently, not to try to overcome Enfield for fear of arousing the other men, against whom – being unarmed – they'd have no chance. No one seemed particularly worried about it, although she had heard Adam tell John Olson that he hoped they'd seen the last of the gang and that they would not try to get even.

But Sharon's thoughts dwelt neither on her foster parents nor on the outlaws, but on Adam Gann. She simply could not understand him. She was convinced from the way she'd caught him looking at her, that she was attractive to him and that he was more than just casually interested, yet he continually rebuffed her – actually rejected her efforts to become better acquainted.

What was wrong? What was the reason for his actions? It wasn't that he had a wife or that there was another woman somewhere whom he intended to marry one day; and he wasn't shy or standoffish as many men were. Why, then, did he so persistently avoid her?

Moody, puzzled, Sharon continued to gaze off across the land as the team slogged steadily on. They were moving through a sort of endless, shallow valley, she had noted, with mountains rising up on both sides in the distance. The air was hot and dry, and the grass covering the baked ground looked withered and dead under the driving sunlight which glistened off the large rocks and shone dully in the gravely stretches occasionally encountered.

There was very little life to be seen; a hawk or two sailing across the cloudless, amazingly blue sky, some sort of small bird that hovered about the weirdly shaped cactus plants; a long-eared jackrabbit that refused to be frightened by their passage and run, but pantingly remained in the shade of a low, glossy-leafed brush.

She would like to know more about the country, wished that Adam Gann was beside her on the seat as he had been that day after they'd crossed the river. He knew what all the strange shrubs and trees were called, the names of the flowers, and was continually seeing something that she missed – like a rattlesnake coiled under a rock to escape the heat, a shrike storing an insect on a thorn for future use, a herd of antelope racing off into the distance – and drawing her attention to it.

They were not too far from the desert, she'd overheard him tell the men; a few more days in country such as they were crossing and they would be at the Mohave, as he called it.

It was difficult to imagine how the desert could be any worse than this destitute world of treeless, black lava-rock mountains, the plains of starved weeds struggling to survive in the blistered sand, but evidently it was. Yet

Adam had told her that despite its bleakness, it was beautiful when the sun was down.

It came alive then, he said. Flowers, closed tight against the heat during the day, opened wide to spread displays of vivid color on the slopes and in the low places. Dully clothed bushes took on a glow, and the trees – green-bunked paloverdes, the ever-present mesquites, the ironwoods – appeared to draw themselves erect and stand proudly in the hush, while the cactuses – candelabra-like saguaros, chollas, ocotillos, their long, red-tipped stems stirring like wands in the night wind – turned the land into a world of eerie, breathtaking beauty.

It was all there to be seen if a person would take note, he'd said, and she had exacted a promise from him to not let her miss any of it.

But that had been days ago when they were riding side by side on the seat of the wagon. Since then many things had happened and Adam had changed, become even more remote and withdrawn, as if he wanted to stay as far from her as possible. And she suspected him of pushing Rufus at her, although she had told him at the start that she had no intention of marrying Rufus Enfield regardless of what others assumed.

How could she go about drawing Adam to her? It was as if they had once been close, lovers in fact, and then something had come between them – only no such understanding or relationship had ever really existed except in her hopes; but Sharon knew she was feeling just as some woman might who had lost her man.

Sighing deeply, she brushed her sunbonnet back with a free hand, and taking a handkerchief from the pocket of her shirtwaist, dabbed at the perspiration gathered on her forehead. Nightfall was not too far off now, four or five hours, perhaps, until the halt to make camp would be called.

And then would come the worst time of all for her, with Adam nearby, talking, eating a meal that she had probably helped prepare, drinking the chicory she had most likely brewed, and acting almost as if she were not around.

She had reached the end of her string, Sharon decided suddenly. She needed advice, needed to talk to another woman. Tillie Ritter was nearest her age, but Tillie, like Mandy Olson and Flo Price, was still peeved at her for some reason – the blue dress she'd put on that day she supposed it was. Why not turn to Beth again? Although much older, she was still much like a sister.

Twisting about on the seat, Sharon looked back into the shadowy depths of the canvas-topped wagon.

'Beth,' she called, 'do you mind coming up here and talking to me?'

Chapter 18

'Got time to do some listening?' Noah McLeod asked.

Adam, hunched on his heels, a cup of chicory in his hand, glanced up. They had finished supper, an extra-fine meal topped off with a wedge of tasty dried-apple pie, and he had drawn off to one side, as was his habit.

'Sure. Any time.'

Elsewhere in the camp other members of the party were completing their evening meal, or already through, were sitting back enjoying the coolness that night was bringing. It had been a hot day, and all were thankful when the sun finally sank behind the hills to the west and a halt was called.

'You men want another piece of this pie?' Beth called, coming toward them. Beyond her, Sharon was clearing up the dishes and drawing water from the cask with which to wash them along with the pans. 'Won't be fit to eat tomorrow.'

Noah looked questioningly at Gann, who shook his head. 'Obliged, but I couldn't get another bite down, I'm so full. Just can't remember when I had a supper good as that one – was almost like it was a special occasion of some kind.'

Beth smiled, considered him gravely, for a few moments, and then turned away. Noah, settling himself on a rock nearby, reached into a pocket of his windbreaker for pipe and tobacco, began to prepare himself a smoke. From off in the welter of creosote bush and mesquite a coyote yipped impatiently.

'You can have vittles like that every day if you're of a mind,' McLeod said, tamping brown shreds of tobacco into the bowl of the blackened briar.

Adam swallowed the last of his chicory coffee, grinned. 'I reckon that's one good thing about being a farmer, a man's always got plenty to eat.'

'Most of the time,' Noah agreed, and added, 'it's a mighty good life – hard, sure, but a man gets back a'plenty if he ain't scared of working. He has his woman and his family with him all the time, so's there ain't never no loneliness. And he's got the ground to work with, make come alive with the seed he's planted – and all the while he can be raising himself some fine stock. There's a lot of satisfaction in farming.'

Gann made no comment, his carefully shaded eyes on Sharon as she moved about the camp. Again she had laid aside the cast-off clothing of her father and was wearing a dress, one of some sort of flowered material

134

that was nipped in at the waist and set off her figure to its best.

It seemed to him that she became more desirable with each passing day, which was making it more difficult to keep her from filling his mind; and McLeod wasn't helping matters any by pointing out the advantages of having a wife and subscribing to a way of life where they could be together continually.

'You aim to keep right on drifting around, punching cattle and the like?' Noah asked.

No, I aim to keep clear of the law, Gann knew he should say, and go into detail concerning his situation, his plans for crossing over the border where he would be safe, after which he would get in touch with Tim Aubrey at the Turkey Track and ask him to use his influence with the governor – but he couldn't bring himself to bare the truth.

He didn't feel that he was lying – lying wasn't in Adam Gann. It was simply a matter of not going into his predicament and revealing that he had been branded a criminal and faced ten years in prison for his crime. It was pure rationalization, but honest and without guile.

'Reckon so. Haven't thought much about changing.'

Adam paused. Rufus Enfield strolled up, spoke casually to Noah and to him, and moved on to where Sharon was now sitting on one of the benches McLeod had built, in conversation with Beth. Halting in front of the girl, he took a moment to adjust the position of his holstered gun, making quite a point of it.

Rufus had said nothing to him about receiving the weapon and there had been no thanks forthcoming for the favor – not that it was important. Rufus would have gotten a pistol anyway, as there were several among the weapons they had taken from the gang of busters. Of course, Daniel Price, evidently never on good terms with his brother-in-law, and hoping to improve relations, may not have mentioned where the gear had come from, simply taking credit for it himself.

'If you ain't minding me saying it,' McLeod continued bluntly, 'it's about time you were doing some thinking about it. Every time that sun comes up a man's a day older, and there sure ain't no way to go back, get younger.'

'For sure,' Adam murmured, eyes still on Sharon and Enfield, who was now attempting to demonstrate his dexterity in drawing his pistol and having little luck... Rufus was the man for her, he told himself; he had no dark clouds hanging over him, was steady, and one of her kind.

'You willing to listen to an offer?'

Gann brought his attention back to Noah. He frowned. 'That what you wanted to talk to me about – an offer?'

'Yes,' McLeod said. 'We've all took a shine to you, and we know what kind of a man you are. I'd like it if you'd throw in with me – us – come on to California or Oregon with us, whichever we decide on. Can build us a fine farm – a real jim dandy – if we work together.'

Did Sharon have a hand in the offer Mc-Leod was making? Adam wondered, thinking back now over the times in the past couple of days when he'd seen the two talking quietly; and there was the excellent meal he'd just enjoyed, and the increasing fatherly interest and attention Noah was according him.

He mulled the proposition about in his mind, savoring all the happiness and contentment such an arrangement would bring – making Sharon his wife if she were willing, putting an end to wandering, sending down roots and building a home and a future, but it was not for him.

Even if they continued on to the high country of Oregon, the law would still track him down and demand that he pay up with ten years of his life for the killing of J. W. Tucker. Likely he would be able to clear himself of the death of Frank Slawson since the men of the wagon train had witnessed the incident with the renegade Apaches, but there would be ten long years in Yuma ahead of him, regardless. And most of all, in the eyes of Sharon and Noah McLeod, and all the other members of the train who had come to mean so much to him, he would be a criminal, a common outlaw.

'What do you say? We got us a deal?'

Adam faced McLeod. The older man had removed his pipe from between his teeth and was studying him intently, hopefully.

'Can see my daughter's took your eye,' he continued. 'Now, I don't mind telling you I'd be proud to have you as my son-in-law. Wife feels the same, and while I got my hunches about it, I reckon you better find out first-hand from Rose Sharon how she feels.'

Gann stirred wearily. 'It's all mighty tempting, Noah,' he said, 'but I just ain't ready yet.'

McLeod nodded slowly, pointed with the stem of his pipe at Sharon and Rufus Enfield, still in conversation near the wagon. 'Best you don't hang back too long. Rufus there's been mighty attentive lately, ever since we run into you, in fact.'

'He's a good man,' Gann murmured.

'That he is… Now, why don't you hold off making up your mind for a bit longer? I expect I can keep Rufus sort of toned down for a while. You said you'd see us to that crossing on the Colorado River, then go your own way. Now, how'd it be if you was to wallow my offer around in your head till we got there – be a week or so the way you figure it – and then give me a yes or no?'

Adam rose. 'Likely be the same,' he said, 'but that's what I'll do.' He started to turn away, hesitated, and looking back at McLeod, extended his hand.

'I'm obliged to you, Noah. Can't tell you how much your offer, and the things you said, mean to me. Good night.'

'G'night,' McLeod responded as Gann moved off.

Chapter 19

Despite his determination not to involve Sharon McLeod in his troubles, Gann could not help but think of her, and of Noah's offer, many times in the succeeding days and nights. And the fact that they were being thrown together more often as the wagons were beginning to break down after the long journey from Virginia forcing the train to halt for necessary repairs, did not help matters any for him.

He did his best to avoid her without doing so obviously or impolitely, always finding a plausible excuse to leave when it appeared they might be alone together for a few minutes. Many times he noticed Sharon frown, puzzled by his actions, but she never seemed to hold it against him, displaying instead a sort of resigned patience as if waiting until some particular day or point was reached.

If that was when the party arrived at the Colorado, and he suspected it was, just as he was sure now that Noah had been induced by his wife – probably without Sharon's knowledge – to make him the partnership offer, he hoped McLeod had let it be known there was small chance of his changing his initial refusal. It would be easier on all if they more or less expected him to decline.

Rolling the problem about in his mind as he rode on a good quarter-mile ahead of the train, Adam let his gaze search the country around them. He had expected to hear from the busters again, seeking recovery of their weapons as well as revenge, but as time had worn on and the wagon train moved farther from their customary haunts, he began to think they need fear no longer.

As they worked their way across the blistered land, however, leaving danger of one sort behind, they approached another. Bandits were common along the fringe of the desert – some being disgruntled hangers-on left over from the large *haciendas,* which had ceased to exist after this stretch of country, once a Mexican possession, became a part of the United States; others coming out of Mexico, crossing the border into Arizona and ranging northward to raid along the routes customarily followed by travelers.

Several times the army had moved in to halt the depredation, but the lawless activity would cease only for the time the soldiers were present. Once they pulled out, returning to Fort Yuma or one of the other posts established in the area, it would all begin again.

There had been no sign of riders anywhere to the west or south, which was where the outlaws could be expected to come from. The rocky, barren hills in the north along which the train was presently skirting, being both waterless and treeless and therefore holding no attraction for those who wished to halt, were usually ignored by the *bandidos,* who preferred to lay their ambuscades in more congenial areas where pilgrims were likely to stop.

The outlaws' preference was easily understandable. The low hills through which they were passing were sandy, supporting little grass. Here and there grotesque Joshua trees stood at lonely attention, surrounded by their lesser kin, the chollas and the yuccas.

In the arroyos, sometimes faced in red, other times in chalk-white soil, desert broom, snakeweed, mescal, and an occasional smoke tree, all looking as if water had not touched them in years, grew at ragged intervals, each not encroaching upon the small, sandy-soiled domain of the other as they fought for survival.

The rocks of the nearby mountains, unnamed so far as Gann knew, were black and glistened in the pitiless rays of the sun. Nothing lived within the mass of smooth-surfaced boulders, for the heat absorbed by the formation during the day turned it into a furnace and made life unbearable.

The train should be all right until they drew nearer to the Colorado; then it would be wise for all to have their weapons handy and keep their eyes peeled for riders appearing abruptly on the crest of a rise, then disappearing just as suddenly. He'd better remember to caution McLeod and the others to that effect when they halted for night camp.

And that time wasn't far off, he saw, glancing toward the sun. Another hour and it would be dropping behind the irregular horizon in the west. It wouldn't be a good camp. There would be no stream or spring along which to stop, no trees to offer shade, no grass to satisfy the horses. They were in the desert's scope, and while not actually on that vast expanse known as the Mohave, they were near, and there was but little difference.

Gann stiffened. Raising a hand, he brushed the sweat from his eyes. Squinting to minimize the glare, he studied a distant rise. A horseman had appeared. Silhouetted against the burning blue of the sky, distorted by intervening waves of shimmering heat, the rider was a solitary figure in the broad, empty land for a long minute.

And then he was no longer alone. Other horsemen began to appear on either side of him, rising into view abruptly as if springing into being like the dragons' teeth sowed by Jason in his search for the golden fleece.

At once Gann cut his horse about, and

hammering at the animal's ribs with his spurless heels, pressed him into a fast gallop for the wagons.

McLeod saw him coming, recognized the signs of trouble, and coming upright, lifted his hand as a signal to the others for a halt. The wagons behind him pulled in close, stopped, the men climbing down and hurrying forward.

'Outlaws!' Gann shouted as he rushed up. Twisting about, he pointed to the ragged line of riders now racing across the low hills and flats toward them. 'Mexican *bandidos*, likely!'

McLeod had resumed his seat, staring at the distant horsemen. 'Mexicans? We that close to Mexico?'

'Couple of days, maybe some less. Way they ride, miles don't mean much to them.'

Sharon and Beth had come from the interior of the wagon and were now crouched in the arch of its canvas top watching the approaching outlaws. The attention of the other women of the train undoubtedly was also focused on the new danger presenting itself.

'I reckon we can handle them,' Rufus Enfield declared, patting the pistol on his hip. 'We've got plenty of guns, now. Bullets, too.'

'The boy's right,' Price agreed.

McLeod looked questioningly at Gann.

'What'd we best do? Sure hate to get caught out here on the flat.'

'Only choice we've got is to head into that mountain,' Adam replied, indicating the glistening mass to the right of the road. 'Not going to be comfortable, but there's nothing else close enough.'

'Don't look much like a mountain,' Olson said. 'More like a big pile of rocks.'

'Just what it is,' Gann said, glancing at the *bandidos*. They were beginning to take on more definite shape now as the distance separating them narrowed. 'The heat'll be something fierce, but we'll be able to make a stand – and against a bunch as big as that, that's what we need.'

Noah McLeod lifted the reins, nodding crisply to the men gathered at the side of his wagon.

'All right – let's get over there and get set,' he said, and bucked his head at Adam as the others wheeled and hurried back to their wagons. 'Lead the way.'

Chapter 20

Gann, bent low over his saddle as he led the train at a fast run for the rocks, endeavored to recall the arrangement of the sprawling formation. He had been there once, and then only briefly, but as near as he could recall, a fairly large, sandy-floored arroyo gashed its east side. He had not explored the area and so had no idea how far back the wash extended, but he did seem to remember that it narrowed into a steep-walled canyon.

Again dashing sweat from his eyes, Adam threw his glance to the outlaws. They were closing in fast; the wagons would barely make it to the mountain in time – and then only if no mishap occurred to slow them down.

The formation loomed before him – shining black rocks, scorched weeds dying in the murderous heat, white sand glittering in the hard sunlight. He had been right, he saw, slowing his horse. The arroyo was there, near the center of the mountain's east face – wide where it met the mesa, narrowing as it curved a course back into the heart of the formation.

Except for the killing heat, no better place could be found to stand off the outlaws, and Gann was thankful they had been near and not far out on the open desert where they could have done nothing but halt and use the wagons as a fortification.

He reached the mouth of the canyon and drew up, his horse sucking wildly for wind after the fast run. He could feel the heat emanating from the rocks, realizing that it would be terrible back in the depths of the mountain; but it should start to break soon. The sun would be gone in another hour or so.

The wagons, bumping and jolting as they rushed over the uneven ground, were rattling noisily as they approached. McLeod, in the lead as was customary, was hunched forward on the seat, lines slack in his hands as he gave his team their heads. Sharon and Beth, barely visible in the canvas arch, were close behind him, on their knees apparently as they gripped the sides of the bed in an effort to keep from being tossed about as the vehicle rocked and careened wildly.

The others, almost obscured by dust, were following closely – the Olsons, the Ritters, and the Prices bringing up the rear. Daniel Price, whip in hand, standing with knees partly bent to absorb the erratic motion of his wagon, was having a difficult time keeping pace.

Adam looked again to the oncoming out-laws, now less than half a mile distant. The wagons would make it. Relief coursed through Gann, and riding on into the arroyo, he swing aside and waited for McLeod to draw even. As the wagon veered into the wash, the left wheels struck a half-buried rock. The vehicle reeled drunkenly, setting up a clatter of pans, and then righting itself, hurried on.

'Keep going – far as you can!' Adam shouted as Noah turned strained features to him.

The older man bobbed in understanding, urged his team on. John Olson, face set to grim lines also, nodded as he passed. The others rushed on by – horses sweat-soaked and caked with dust, their own skins and clothing showing damp spots and covered with a tan film, wagons cracking and pop-ping in protest.

As the last of the train passed, Gann rode back into the center of the wash and halted. The outlaws, now close, were definite figures as they spurred their horses toward the mountain. With their high-crowned and curled wide-brimmed hats, bits of silver flashing from their gear, they could only be, as he had suspected, bandits from across the border.

There was an even dozen of them. Adam swore feelingly. It was fortunate the train had been so near the massive rock formation when spotted by the *bandidos;* a mile or two farther away and the Mexicans would have intercepted them in the open.

Wheeling, Gann headed back up the sandy wash, feeling the sweat oozing from every pore in his body with each passing moment. The arroyo began to narrow as the rock walls to either side closed in. Boulders, some as large as one of the wagons, lined the edges of the cleft, having tumbled down into the gash at some time in the past during one of the tumultuous storms that infrequently lashed the area, or perhaps earlier when there had occurred a mighty upheaval in the earth. That the train had barely made it through between them in places was evidenced by scrape marks.

McLeod, with Price and the other men, abruptly appeared ahead. Faces sober, weathered skin glistening with moisture, each carrying a weapon, they came down the arroyo at a trot. Adam wheeled in behind one of the large boulders, came off the saddle. The men halted before him.

'Can't go no farther,' McLeod said. 'This here wash leads into a kind of a yard and ends. We've got the wagons lined up in there.'

'This must be what hell's like,' Daniel Price muttered, mopping at his neck with a bandanna. He glanced toward the approaching outlaws, now almost at the mouth of the arroyo. 'What's the plan?'

'Stand them off,' Gann answered. 'First thing's to see what they'll do.'

'They'll bottle us up – in fact that's what they've already done,' Olson said. 'We're in a trap.'

'Beats getting caught out there on the flats,' McLeod snapped. 'But this ain't no time to be bickering.' He turned to Gann. 'What do you want us to do?'

Adam, pulling his rifle from the saddle boot, said, 'Stay with your wagons. I don't know if there's a way into here from the other side of the mountain or not. Best we figure there is and be ready.'

'Looks like nothing but cliffs and bald knobs,' Ritter said. 'Could be a trail up there, however. What are you figuring to do?'

'Hole up behind this rock. Can stop any of them trying to come down the wash.'

McLeod said, 'Good idea. One of us can stay here – side you–'

'No need,' Adam said. 'Be better for you to stick close to the women and the wagons. If the Mexicans can get in from the back side, it'll take all of you to hold them off.'

McLeod nodded and started back up the arroyo with the others. It was better that way. None of the men was particularly familiar with the weapons taken from the busters, being more experienced with shotguns, which were effective only at a moderate range, and such would be the way of it if the *bandidos* attempted to close in from above.

Crouched behind the boulder, rifle in hand, Adam watched the outlaws sweep up to the mouth of the wash and draw to a sliding, dusty stop. Horses champing on the bit, fidgeting nervously, the Mexicans considered the arroyo while talking back and forth. Abruptly a yell went up from them and the entire party, slashing at the flanks of their mounts with long-tined spurs, rushed into the arroyo.

Gann raised his rifle, and careful not to touch the searing surface of the boulder with his arm, took aim on the nearest of the outlaws and pressed off a shot. The Mexican jolted, reeling on his saddle as the bullet drove into him. Scarcely noting, Adam levered a fresh load into the chamber of his weapon, drew bead again on another outlaw, and quickly triggered a second shot. As the man sagged, caught at the oversized horn of his saddle to keep from falling, his friends opened up with their weapons and bullets began to ricochet off the rock and send up spurts of sand nearby.

But the oncoming line slowed, faltered. Again Adam jacked a cartridge into place, fired. The bandit he was leveling at wheeled in that exact instant. The bullet only grazed him, but it sent him racing back for the mouth of the arroyo. At once the others, taking their cue from him, followed.

Gann's taut shape relented slightly. He lowered his weapon and watched from the shelter of the rock as the outlaws drew off, well out of range, to assess their situation. What they did next would determine which course he and the men of the wagon train would now follow.

He hoped the Mexican *bandidos* would come to the conclusion that four wagons were not worth the effort, and the cost already paid in the wounding of two of their members – but there was no way of anticipating their decision. He could only wait and see.

Chapter 21

The outlaws, stringing out across the mouth of the arroyo, began to dismount. Allowing their reins to drop to the ground, they pushed their hats to the backs of their heads and squatted on the hot sand. Gann could not see what had happened to the pair he'd shot. Likely they were among the others being attended to, and he wondered how seriously wounded they were. He had aimed to kill, but the rifle, strange to him, evidently shot a bit off target.

Adam heard a sound behind him, pivoted quickly. It was Sharon. Features drawn with concern, dusty, clothing stained, she hurried up to him, paused.

'I – we wanted to see if you were all right,' she said. 'We heard the shooting and–'

Adam grinned as her words trailed off. He was pleased to think she would worry about him but reminded himself it would be best to keep matters on a purely friend-of-the-family basis.

'Safe here behind this big rock,' he said. 'Any problems back at the wagons?'

The stiffness of his attitude was not lost to her. She nodded. 'No, except for the heat.

It's terrible back in there – like an oven.'

'It'll start cooling off a bit soon,' he said.

She was craning her neck, looking beyond him at the outlaws. 'What are they doing?'

'Seem to've settled down. Going to wait us out, I expect.'

She glanced about. 'That shooting – were they trying to follow us into here?'

'Tried,' Gann said. 'Your pa and the others able to look for another trail into the box?'

'They can't do much – the rocks are so hot,' she replied, 'but they were able to look around some. Didn't find anything.' Sharon paused, came about, and faced him squarely. 'What will happen to us if we're trapped in here?'

Gann's shoulders stirred. Two of the *bandidos* had mounted and were riding off to the south. The wounded ones, he guessed, pulling out. The odds had dropped slightly, but still not enough to make a difference.

'We're not going to stay trapped for long,' he said, hoping to reassure the girl. 'We'll figure a way out. We're all right so far. They can't get to us, so it's a standoff.'

'But they can keep us in here until we're forced to give in,' Sharon said, brushing at a wisp of hair coming down over an eye. 'That won't take very long. We can't stand a whole day of heat like this.'

Gann made no reply, thus admitting to the truth of her words. Although nightfall was

154

not far off, the temperature in the rocks was extreme – unbelievably high, in fact, though considerably lower than during the day when the sun was overhead.

'Good chance we'll be out of here by morning, early,' Adam said, keeping his attention on the outlaws. They were yet at ease, seemingly interested in doing nothing more than whiling away time. 'When you get back to the wagons, I'll be obliged if you'll tell your pa and the others that I'd like to talk.'

Sharon again brushed at a stray lock. 'All right,' she said in a lifeless sort of voice that reflected her concern for their situation. 'Best I go now – I slipped off without anyone knowing – but there's actually no danger while we're in here, is there?'

'No. Long as they stay where they are, we're out of range.'

He let it drop there, seeing no reason to worry her further by mentioning the possibility of the Mexicans circling around after the rocks were cool enough to crawl over, and trails or not, coming over the top of the mountain at them. He'd discuss that with McLeod and the other men, along with an idea that had taken shape in his mind.

Sharon gave him a brief smile, murmured 'Be careful,' and turning, hurried off.

He watched her start back up the wash, again moved to think that she had cared enough to see if he was all right. He wished he could have shown his feelings, let her know how much it meant to him, but he dared not – at least not at the moment. Later, he decided grimly, if matters worsened and it appeared none of them would see the light of day, he would tell her how he really felt.

Once more he put his attention on the outlaws. Shadows were now beginning to stretch out from the foot of the mountain, and some of the Mexicans were already enjoying relief from the sun. It would be somewhat cooler out there in the open; the faint wind that ordinarily sprang up at sunset, would touch them, but back in the box 'a kind of a yard,' Noah had termed it – in the center of the mountain of rocks, there would be no change, for the breeze would never reach there.

The dry scuff of boots brought Gann around again. McLeod, with the other men of the wagon train close about him, came in sight. Features strained beneath a coating of sweat and dust, they came up quickly.

'Ain't no trails coming in that we can find,' McLeod said as they halted behind the rock. 'And there ain't no way out, 'cepting right back through this wash. Olson was right – we're in a trap.'

'And a mighty damned hot one!' Ritter said, mopping at his neck. 'My wife and boy are suffering plenty.'

'Everybody is,' Noah said, peering around the rock at the outlaws. 'We're all roasting and they're laying out there, taking it easy. You got any idea what they're aiming to do?'

'Can bet on one thing,' Adam said. 'They won't be trying anything until it cools off.'

McLeod sleeved sweat from his streaming face. 'Well, no matter, we sure've got to do something before morning. Can't stand a whole day of heat like this.'

'How about us rushing them?' Rufus Enfield suggested, taking a turn at studying the bandits. 'Looks like there ain't no more'n a dozen of them out there.'

'Only ten,' Gann said, 'but we'd never get near enough to do any good. They'd cut us down before we got halfway.'

'Then what'll we do?' Price demanded wearily, brushing at his eyes. Shadows were beginning to form on the side of the mountain as the sun sank lower.

'Maybe we ought to try figuring out what they're going to do,' Daniel Price commented, his gaze on half a dozen vultures soaring lazily high overhead in the sky, still bright with sunlight.

'Good chance they won't do anything but wait us out,' Adam said, 'but we can't bank on it. They could try charging us again, hoping to get through to the box, or they might swing around and come at us from the top of the mountain—'

'Still saying it was a mistake to come in here,' Olson grumbled, and hastily raised a hand to stay Noah McLeod's sharp retort. 'I know we wouldn't've had much chance out there on the flats, either, but maybe if we'd pulled the wagons into a tight circle—'

'They would've killed your horses first off and pinned you down same as we are in here,' Gann said. 'What I think we ought to do is not wait for them to make a move, but go for help.'

'Go where for help?' McLeod said in a dispirited tone. 'It's a thousand miles to anywhere.'

'There's a mining town called Wickenburg north and east of here, near as I recollect.'

'How far?' Ritter asked anxiously.

'Half a day, maybe a bit more – not too sure of that. It's a fair-sized place and usually there's army around. If not, there may be a US marshal or a sheriff and plenty of men who'll pitch in and make up a posse.'

'I'll go,' Rufus said at once.

McLeod glanced at him, and then at Daniel Price. The latter nodded slightly, giving his approval.

McLeod said, 'That's good. Best Gann stays here. He's the only one of us who knows how to deal with them renegades.'

Olson spat, wiped his heat-cracked lips. 'All right. Sounds good – but how's Rufus going to get out of here? Sure as hell can't take a horse over the mountain, and he can't get by them outlaws without being seen.'

'We'll have to try,' Adam said. 'Soon as it's full dark, we'll make the move. Meantime, Rufus, get a horse ready.'

'Can ride that spare of mine,' Jim Ritter offered. 'He ain't worked today and will be in good shape.'

'Still don't see how we can get Rufus past them Mexicans.'

It was Price. Gann shook his head at the man. 'Be up to us to keep them busy while he's trying,' he said. 'I've been watching them close. They're strung out across the arroyo like they might try riding in again. What I figure will work is, after dark we'll move as far up the wash – along the right-hand side – as we can without them seeing us. Rufus will be with us, only on the left side.

'The rocks are higher on the right and they're bigger and there's a lot more of them near the mouth of the arroyo. We'll work our way into them, and when the time's right, we'll start in shooting at the Mexicans. It'll draw them to us, and that'll be the sign for Rufus to slip out and head for Wickenburg.'

'Going to take some mighty careful doing,' Price said, doubtfully. 'You sure you can handle it, Rufus?'

Enfield said, 'I can do it, Daniel. Don't

fret none over it.'

'It's our only hope,' McLeod said, 'and Rufus is the only one of us young enough to make a hard ride fast and get us some help.'

'I'll make it,' Rufus assured them again. 'How soon do you reckon it'll be before I can leave?'

'Another hour,' Gann replied. 'It's got to be full dark.'

'I'll be ready,' Enfield said, and wheeling, headed back for the wagons.

McLeod watched him for a moment and then said: 'Reckon we all'd better be getting set. Adam, you want somebody to spell you here for a bit?'

Gann shook his head. 'As soon wait here as anywhere. See you all at dark.'

Chapter 22

Near dark Sharon came again, this time bringing a plate of food and a cup of strong, black chicory. Adam thanked the girl for her thoughtfulness, but conversation between them was strained. When he had finished his meal, she took the empty utensils, and with only a quiet smile, returned to the box.

Adam tried not to think of her as he took up a stand at the side of the boulder where he could maintain a constant surveillance over the outlaws. They were as they had been, sprawled out across the mouth of the arroyo, some apparently sleeping, others idling away the time playing a game that involved flipping coins while their horses waited, hipshot, beyond them.

Were they, too, holding off until nightfall before making their move? If so, what could be their plan? Another straight-on charge such as they had attempted at the start? Adam doubted that. It had proved too costly.

Perhaps they did know of another way into the heart of the mountain and were delaying until the time was right to make use of it. Adam admitted he was not well acquainted with the formation, had but a slight, passing knowledge of it. There could be another trail in.

Darkness was complete. Two or three fires now glowed, like small, red eyes in the night, at the end of the arroyo. No doubt they had been started to keep the area alight so that anyone attempting an escape would be quickly detected. They would not be troubling to cook, he was certain of that. They would have brought with them prepared food – jerky, corn tortillas, and the like.

A thread of satisfaction moved through Adam. The outlaws were expecting them to make a try at breaking out. Such would make the diversion he planned all the more effective.

'Gann?'

McLeod's voice, hushed for no good reason other than the tenseness of their position, as they were well beyond earshot of the bandits, came to him at the same instant as he heard the sound of the men's arriving.

'Right here,' he replied.

Noah, with Price, Ritter, and Olson, eased up into the darker shadow of the rock. Adam glanced beyond them.

'Where's Rufus?'

'He's coming,' Price replied and jerked a thumb in the general direction of the box.

McLeod said, 'Plenty dark enough now. Sure oughtn't to wait much longer.'

'Can start any time,' said Adam, his

impatience beginning to build as Enfield still failed to put in his appearance. *'Ban-didos* have built themselves some fires to light up the mouth of the arroyo.'

'That bad or good?' Olson wondered, stretching to see past the boulder.

'I figure it's good,' Gann said, and grunted with relief as Rufus, leading his horse, emerged from the darkness. 'I think they're sort of expecting us to make a run for it tonight, and will all come running over to the south side when we start a ruckus.'

'Now when we do, Rufus, you just can't jump on that horse and go riding out of here,' Price warned. 'You do and you'll have a couple of them chasing after you. What you've got to do is stay down low, lead your horse out, then when you're off in the dark, mount up and ride.'

'I know what I've got to do, Daniel,' Enfield said peevishly. 'That town, Wickenburg – it's northeast of here?'

Gann said, 'Yes – maybe a bit more east than north.'

'You know which way's north?' Price asked, an edge of scorn to his voice. 'Stars ain't easy to follow.'

'He's got my compass,' Olson said. 'He'll do all right.'

'I'm hoping,' Price muttered.

Adam's attention was on the outlaws. The fires still burned, and while the men were no

163

longer distinct, he could see shadowy figures moving about in the glow of the flames.

'Expect it's time,' he said, brushing at the sweat misting his eyes. The oppressive heat had abated but little. 'Everybody set?'

There was a murmur of assent. Gann turned to Rufus. 'Start working your way along this side of the wash as soon as we move off. When you get about halfway, or a bit farther, hold up. Then, when the shooting starts and you see the outlaws all heading for the other side, move out. Like Daniel said, keep low and lead your horse till you're in the clear.'

Rufus was nodding his head even before Gann had finished. 'I know what I'm to do,' he said somewhat stiffly.

'Maybe so, but we all had better understand just how it's to be because we sure can't let anything go wrong. You're our only chance. They'll be coming at us in the morning – maybe sooner. I figure we can hold them off for a while if we know help's on the way.'

McLeod swore deeply. 'Hell of a spot to be in! What the devil do they want to bother us for? Ain't much cash money on us, and the stuff we're carrying – the clothes and furniture and such – don't amount to shucks.'

'Guns, horses, but mainly the women – that's what they're after,' Adam explained.

'The women?' Olson repeated.

Gann nodded. 'Once they're done with them, they'll take them down into Mexico, sell them to a brothel. American women bring a high price.'

Jim Ritter rubbed at his jaw nervously. 'Well, they ain't getting my wife! It'll be over my dead body.'

'Goes for me, too,' Olson said.

Again Adam glanced at the outlaws as the low conversation between the wagon train men continued. He could see no change. 'Let's get at it,' he said abruptly, and bending low, stepped out from behind the boulder where he had maintained his vigil and hurried to the opposite side of the arroyo.

Reaching there, he halted, looked to see if McLeod and the others were with him. They were, had formed a short line close to the rock wall of the wash. He heard Olson swear, guessing the man had thoughtlessly laid his hand against one of the boulders. There was still enough heat stored within them after the hours of blazing sun to sear the skin despite the advent of night.

'You're all armed?' Gann said, believing he knew the answer but wanting to be sure. Ritter had once intimated that he'd have nothing to do with a gun – not ever.

'Pistols,' McLeod said. 'Talked it over. Could've brought rifles or scatterguns, but we figured a pistol would be easier to handle. We ain't aiming to do much more than raise a rumpus, are we?'

Gann was studying the outlaws closely. He could see them more plainly now at that shorter distance. Several had stretched out on the sand and were asleep. At least two appeared to be on guard duty – both hunkered on their heels facing the arroyo, their backs to the fire so as to not be blinded by the glare.

'Every one of them that you can put a bullet in means one less to deal with later,' Adam said, answering McLeod, and moved forward. 'Stay up close to the rocks. After things get to going and you hear me holler "Back", that'll be the signal to start heading back to the wagons.'

There was a murmur of understanding, and Gann, with his men following in single file, began to work his way along the south bank of the arroyo. He had taken only scant notice of that side earlier, was now searching for a break in the wall that would permit him and the others to climb higher into the boulders.

It came shortly. He paused as he started to lead the way up the gully. They were fairly near the outlaws now.

'No talking,' he cautioned in a low whisper. 'And watch your step. Kick a rock loose and the ball will open before we're ready.'

'Going to be hard to be careful,' Olson said as they moved on. 'Damned rocks are still so hot a man can hardly touch them.'

Gann, crouched to keep as low a silhouette as possible, placing each foot carefully and steadying himself with a hand placed against a convenient boulder while ignoring the pain, pressed on. The others, equally cautious, were dark shadows dogging his heels.

Abruptly a stone dislodged by one of them, or by the gradual cooling that was setting in, broke loose from its position and bounded nosily down the slope to stop on the floor of the wash. Instantly a yell went up from one of the sentries, and the entrance to the arroyo was suddenly alive with men leaping to their feet, shouting questions.

'Damn,' McLeod muttered, 'we've gone and spoiled Rufus's chances—'

'Maybe not,' Gann replied in a whisper. 'Fan out and start shooting at them.'

The men began to separate on the steep grade, working in behind the larger rocks. Shortly they began to shoot at the outlaws.

The Mexicans, now aware of where the problem lay, began hurrying toward the south side of the wash, dropping low and angling off into the shadows beyond the firelight as they opened up on the slope.

Gann, keeping an eye on the north wall of the wash, ready to draw a bead on any of the outlaws who might be concentrating his attention on that point, dropped flat to the ground as bullets began to thud into the rocks or ricochet and scream off into the night.

Watching closely, he finally saw faint movement in the darkness along the opposite bank of the wash – nothing more than a blur of motion which caught his attention briefly and then was gone. But that was all Adam needed. Rufus had made it, was now on his way.

'Back!' he yelled, raising his voice to be heard above the rattle of gunshots, and then began a slow, careful retreat among the rocks.

The others ceased firing, and when it became apparent to the outlaws that shots were no longer coming from the slope, they too, believing they had thwarted an attempt on the part of the pilgrims to escape, put away their weapons.

Reaching the floor of the wash, Gann waited in the darkness for the others to appear. They came in one by one, worn, cursing the heated rocks, but relieved and happy when told that Rufus Enfield had managed to get clear without being seen and was on his way to Wickenburg.

'You figure this'll end it for the night, or are they liable to do something?' Ritter wondered as they moved back down the wash.

'We'll know in a few minutes,' Gann replied. 'If they don't rush us now, we can bank on them waiting until daylight.'

'That'll be so's they can see to get around in them rocks above us,' McLeod said. 'Leastwise, that's how I look at it. All they're aiming to do tonight is keep us boxed up in here.'

'Probably right,' Price agreed, 'and it makes sense. Why would they take a chance on slipping and busting their asses and burning their hides on them boulders now when all they've got to do is wait for daylight – and we sure ain't going nowheres in the meantime.'

'For sure,' Noah McLeod muttered as they reached the rock where Gann had established his position. 'Adam, you want us to hang around in case they take a notion to try something?'

'No need,' Gann said. 'Go on back to your wagons and get some sleep. I'll keep an eye open – and fire off a shot if it looks like they're coming in.'

'You sure you ain't too tired?'

'I'm in good shape,' Adam said, and watched the men turn and trudge wearily off into the darkness.

They were grown men, all older than he, but he wasn't absolutely sure they understood the desperate situation they were in. Or else, for the very reason of being older, they could be accepting whatever lay ahead in that matter-of-fact way of those who respect but have ceased to fear death.

And death could be how it would end for all of them, Adam Gann realized as he settled down on the slowly cooling sand to watch the outlaws. Their sole hope was to hold out until help arrived – and that must happen by mid-morning at the latest. If it did not come by then, their chances for survival would slide downward from slim to none.

Chapter 23

The night passed slowly and without interruption. Gann, dozing fitfully beside the boulder, kept the outlaws under surveillance as best he could with the aid of their fires. It was not until the first pearly flare broke the darkness in the east that he noted changes taking place.

The Mexicans began to stir, get to their feet, and move about. He watched them closely, saw several drop back to where the horses were standing.

Drawing himself upright, Adam kept his eyes on them as they mounted and swung back into the center of the camp. They gathered there, four men in the saddle silhouetted above the others in the murky light, and then the quartet of riders separated, two moving off to the left of the arroyo, two taking an opposite course.

Immediately Gann pivoted and ran to the box where the wagons had been pulled into a half circle. McLeod and Price were up, the latter poking about in the fire to get it started. Both wheeled to him as he rushed up.

'What is it?' McLeod demanded. 'Thought you said you'd fire a shot if–'

'Didn't want to let them know I'd seen them,' Gann replied, sucking for wind. 'They've split up. I figure you can look for two of them coming over the top at you from the south side. Another two'll show up on the north. The rest'll probably come down the arroyo, like they tried before.'

'Then we'd best get back there with you – leastwise one of us,' Daniel Price said.

Adam shook his head, turned to retrace his steps. To be gone from his post by the rock too long was risky. Like as not the *bandidos* would not rush him until their friends had reached the rocks above the box canyon and they could attack simultaneously – but he was not taking anything for granted.

'No, you're one man short as it is,' he said. 'And I've got the edge on them – they're coming at me. Best you two and Olson and Ritter scatter out so's you're covering all four sides. That way you can keep an eye on the rocks above you. Might be smart to put the women and children under the wagons... Good luck.'

'Same, and thanks,' McLeod replied as Gann hurried away.

There had been no change in the outlaw camp other than the absence of the four who had ridden off into the early morning gloom. Dropping beside the boulder once again, Adam drew his pistol, checked its loads. Finding it ready, he then thumbed a

172

dozen or so cartridges from the loops of his belt and placed them in a shelflike niche in the side of the rock where they would be quickly available.

Gann turned then to the rifle, jacked it partly open to see if there was a live shell in the chamber. There was, and closing its action, he propped the weapon against his fortification and settled back. He was as ready as he would ever be, he supposed.

He could have more cartridges on hand for the rifle, there being only what was in the magazine; but he reckoned it didn't really matter. He'd probably get a few shots off with the long gun as the outlaws charged, and then it would be a matter of shooting at close quarters, during which the pistol would be more effective.

The minutes dragged on as the sky lightened steadily. Finally the sun broke over the rim of gray-blue mountains to the east and the flats and the mountain became a world of light and shadow.

Abruptly a gunshot shattered the warm hush that dawn had laid across the land. It came from somewhere deep in the rocks above the wagon camp. Gann's jaw hardened. He'd been right. The Mexicans knew of trails that allowed them to gain the higher levels from which they could pour bullets down onto the men below.

More guns began to crackle from the rocks,

and then Adam heard McLeod and the other men open up with a return fire. He turned again to face the outlaws at the far end of the wash. They would be coming now.

The Mexicans were all in the saddle – six of them. That agreed with his careful accounting, which called for him to know exactly the number of *bandidos* they were up against and just where they would be. Originally the party had totaled twelve; he had wounded two, four had circled to the top of the mountain, leaving six who were preparing to race down the wash and close their side of the vise.

They seemed in no hurry, apparently wanting to allow the men above to do as much damage as possible and, hopefully, force all of the wagon train members to make a stand from a single point. They could give that up as far as he was concerned, he thought grimly; he'd be right there behind the rock waiting for them.

The quick beat of running feet brought Gann around. A low curse exploded from his tight lips. It was Sharon. Breathless, face flushed, eyes bright, she hurried up and dropped beside him.

'You want to get yourself killed?' he snapped angrily. 'That bunch is getting ready to charge us! Another few seconds and–'

'Would it have made a difference to you, Adam?' she cut in quietly, looking up into his frowning face.

He pulled away, threw his attention to the bandits. They were lined up at the mouth of the arroyo as if awaiting a signal. Back at the wagon train the shooting had become steady. Picking up his rifle, he spoke without turning to the girl.

'It would, plenty. Now, I've got to get you to the wagons. Not safe here for you.'

'Or there, either,' she said. 'And if I've got to die, I want it to be while I'm with you, Adam.'

A frown wrinkled his brow and his eyes narrowed as if the thought of her dying was occurring to him for the first time. Stubble-covered jaw set, he shook his head.

'I'm not letting that happen,' he said, and lunged upright as the sudden drumming of hoofs filled the wash. The charge was on.

'Keep down low – and close to the rock,' he said in a taut voice, and whipping up the rifle, drew a bead on the first of the outlaws.

The man was bent close over his saddle. When the bullet met him, he seemed to go even lower. His arms dropped limply to the sides of his horse, and then in the next instant he began to fall.

Levering the rifle, Adam fired again, missing as the rider veered. The outlaws were slowing as if surprised to find someone still there midway between them and the box where the wagons had halted.

Jacking the rifle hurriedly, Gann took more deliberate aim at one of the *bandidos,* pressed off a bullet. The Mexican's yell rose above the popping of the guns at the wagon camp, echoed weirdly along the arroyo, and then faded as the man wheeled, and with the others, none of whom had fired a shot, doubled back to the north of the wash.

Adam sank back, turned, levered the rifle for a fresh load. He swore silently. The magazine was empty. He'd have to rely on his pistol when the bandits renewed their charge – and that called for holding his fire until they were almost upon him. Again he swore quietly, this time at the hopelessness of the situation. There were still five of them, one of whom was apparently slightly wounded; at close range he could probably hit two or three of them before they downed him.

Crouched beside the rock, he looked toward the wagons. The shooting had increased there, it seemed, but there was no way to tell if it was on the part of the outlaws or the McLeod party.

He started to say again that he wished she were back with the wagons, but let it drop. Sharon was right. She would be no better off there. Once the outlaws overran him, which they undoubtedly would do on their next attempt, it would be all over for the McLeod party. They would be trapped, with the Mexicans closing in on them from the arroyo as well as from above.

'We don't have a chance, do we, Adam?'

Sharon's voice was low, sober. There was no point in not being honest with her.

'Looks bad, all right. Not much hope of me stopping them again.'

'Maybe Rufus will come with help.'

'Maybe,' Gann said, with no conviction. 'It'll be a long ride to Wickenburg and back. He'll make it, can bet on that. Just could be too late, though.'

Sharon was sitting on the sand, hands in her lap, face tipped down. She had on the same snug-fitting dress that he had admired before, had complemented it now with a poke-berry-dyed scarf wrapped about her head to hold her dark hair in place.

'Adam,' she said softly, 'will you tell me something?'

'Can try.'

'Why do you treat me the way you do?' she said, raising her troubled eyes to him. 'I've done my best to show you how much you mean to me – that I love you – but you push me off, keep me at arm's length. Don't I mean anything to you?'

He was silent for a long breath. Then, 'You do – more'n any woman I've ever known – more'n I thought any woman ever could.'

'Then why–'

There was no reason not to explain. Within only minutes, likely, he would be dead.

'Just this – you'd have no future with me. That man the Apaches killed was not my partner, like your pa and the others thought. He was a U.S. marshal – and he was taking me to Yuma Prison.'

Sharon was staring at him, lips parted, eyes round and filled with surprise. 'Prison!' she echoed.

'I killed a man – rancher. It was a fair fight, but the judge sentenced me to ten years anyway. I'd changed my mind about going ahead and serving out my term and was hunting for a way to escape when those Indians jumped us and killed Slawson. Your pa and the others offering me the job of seeing you on to the Colorado came just at the right time.'

He paused, studying her closely, as if endeavoring to assess her reaction. She was looking at him, a mixture of shock and disbelief in her eyes, and then suddenly she rocked forward, throwing her arms around his neck.

'Oh, Adam!' she cried. 'That doesn't make the slightest difference!'

He held her close, savoring the fleeting moments. And then, 'It should. You can't waste your life on me – an outlaw – a man with a price on his head. Every lawman and bounty hunter in this part of the country's on the lookout for me, now. I'd figured to go to Mexico, hide out there, try to get word to a friend of mine–'

'They'd never find you in Oregon, and that's where you could go if you'd accept Pa's offer. Oregon's a long ways from here.'

Adam gently disengaged himself. 'The law's everywhere in this country. They'd soon catch up with me – and leaving you then would be even harder than it is now.'

He paused, cast a glance at the outlaws. They were preparing to charge again. High above them in the clean, cloudless sky vultures were once more circling patiently, as if waiting.

'The *bandidos* will be coming in a minute or so. I want you to stay far back against this rock, keep out of sight as much as you can. I aim to keep them real busy till my six-gun's empty, so when you see a good chance while that's going on, slip by and go hide somewhere along the arroyo until that posse gets here. They ought–'

Gann's words broke off as the hammer of hoofs again filled the wash. A regretful sort of smile pulled at his mouth. He reached out, took the girl in his arms, and kissed her.

'Expect this is the big wind,' he said, releasing her and stepping quickly to the corner of the boulder. 'It would have been a fine thing, spending my life with you... So long, lady.'

Tears flooded into Sharon's eyes. 'Good-bye,' she murmured, and sank back upon the sand.

Chapter 24

The riders closed in fast, five men hunched low, firing as they came. Bullets thudded against the rock behind which Adam and the girl crouched, some shrieking off into space, others making a dull thunking sound as they struck.

Gann, pistol ready, was aware of the steady shooting still underway back in the box and reckoned McLeod and the others were still holding their own – they could even be succeeding in turning the outlaws back. But that would all go for nothing unless he was able to stop the ones in the arroyo, prevent their getting by him and putting the wagon train people in a cross-fire. Regardless, with a bit of luck, Sharon would come through safely.

The thunder of the approaching horses increased, and dust began to lay a thick, tan blanket between the walls of the arroyo. Adam looked at Sharon. She smiled faintly as he nodded. Moving then to the edge of the boulder, seemingly oblivious of the hail of bullets, he raised his weapon.

The riders were still a few yards too far for effective pistol range – and he must make every shot count; there'd be no chance to reload. He hung there, crouched, rigid, weapon ready. The Mexicans began to yell – wild, nerve-shattering sounds that echoed along the wash and blended with the gun-shots.

Cool, Adam rode out the moments. The first outlaw reached the mark – a jagged bit of white-streaked rock – that he had chosen as a deadline. Steadying his pistol, he squeezed off a shot. The Mexican threw up his hands, began to fall from his horse.

Barely moving, Gann lined up on a second rider. They were close now, no more than a stride or two away. He triggered his weapon, saw the man buckle, his dark face contorted with pain, and tumble from the saddle.

In that next fragment of time the three remaining outlaws were rushing by. Pain stabbed at Gann's face, wrenched at his shoulder. He staggered back flat against the boulder, firing point blank at a man coming straight at him. A broad smear of blood appeared magically on the outlaw's chest. Mouth distended in a soundless yell, he pitched forward on his suddenly balking horse and went full length onto the sand.

Numb, feeling the wet stickiness of blood on his cheek and down his left arm, Gann doggedly forced himself to face the last two Mexicans. He had three cartridges left in the pistol – enough if he took care.

'Adam!'

He came half about, taking his attention from the arroyo with its swirling dust and drifting powder smoke and shying, nervous horses. Sharon was on her feet beside him, gripping his arm tightly. The remaining two Mexicans, hands raised above their heads, had come to a halt nearby. Gann shook his head, not understanding.

'Rufus is back!' the girl cried. 'He got here with help!'

A long sigh escaped Adam's tightly compressed lips.

Holstering his weapon, he pulled wearily away from the boulder and put his gaze on a dozen or so riders moving in. Some were halting, others were spurring on toward the wagons where scattered gunshots could be heard. It was over there, too, apparently. The outlaws up in the rocks could have seen the posse arrive and would be trying to effect an escape.

'You're hurt!' It was Sharon's concerned voice. 'Your face – it's cut. And you've been hit in the arm.'

A man with dark, heavily lined features and wearing the star of a U.S. marshal, rode up. He bobbed curtly and then called out to the members of the posse still there.

'Couple of you fellows – grab them Mexes. Tie them up and bring them on down to the wagon camp.'

'Yes, sir, Marshal!' one replied as the law-man rode on.

'Adam, come on,' Sharon urged, pulling at his hand. 'I've got medicine at the wagon. I want to doctor you up.'

Gann shrugged, stepped out into the center of the arroyo with the girl, and started for the box. The pain had dwindled now to a steady throbbing and he was hardly conscious of it. He'd been lucky, he reckoned; he had only a gash in a cheek from a rock splinter and a bullet through the fleshy part of an arm. He hoped McLeod and the other members of the wagon train had fared as well.

Several men of the posse, in the charge of a young deputy, galloped by just as they reached the boxlike area where the wagons were halted.

'Going after the rest of them renegades!' one shouted.

Adam and Sharon scarcely heard. They were staring ahead to where the pilgrims were gathered at the Olson wagon. Adam swore softly. Someone had been hurt – John Olson, apparently. Together they hurried up. It was as he had guessed. Olson had taken a bullet in the chest, had died shortly there-after. There'd been no other casualties.

Glancing about, Gann saw Rufus standing off to the side with the Prices, and smiled his congratulations and thanks. Enfield dropped his eyes, seemingly avoiding him. At that moment Beth McLeod saw Sharon and Gann, and with a little cry of relief, ran to them.

'You're safe – both of you!' she said, and looked around as Noah, with Ritter and Daniel Price, came up.

'Glad you made it!' McLeod said. 'Both of you! And we're here to thank you, Adam. Hadn't been for the way you outfigured that bunch, we'd not be alive now. You hurt bad?'

Gann, keeping partly turned from the men as he shook hands all around, said, 'Not bad. Reckon we all ought to be thanking Rufus for getting back in time with the posse. Sure wish Olson hadn't run into bad luck.'

McLeod brushed at his dust-covered face. 'A sad thing, all right. Asked me, last thing, to tell you he appreciated all you done for us, and asked a favor.'

Adam frowned. The pain in his arm was beginning to increase now, and the wound in his cheek felt stiff, dry.

'Favor?'

'Said to ask you if you'd see his wife on the rest of the way so's she could settle with us–'

'Afraid Gann ain't going nowhere,' the marshal said, stepping up. 'Bad time for this, I know, but it's best you don't make any plans that include him.'

The sudden hush that fell when the lawman finished speaking was broken only by the crying of the Ritter baby, back in the wagon. McLeod, his sharp, blue eyes narrowing, faced the marshal.

'What're you trying to tell us?'

The lawman jerked a thumb at Rufus. 'Young fellow there that you sent for me recognized the man on a wanted poster in the sheriff's office. His name's Adam Gann–'

'We know who he is,' Price snapped.

The marshal stirred indifferently. 'Well, guess you do, but maybe what you don't know is that he's an outlaw–'

'Outlaw!' McLeod echoed in disbelief. 'You're looney! This man ain't no outlaw!'

Chapter 25

'I know what I'm talking about,' the lawman said quietly.

Adam looked over the heads of the shocked group to Enfield. Rufus was standing apart from the others, face tipped down, unable to meet either his glance or the angry ones being shunted at him by the wagon train members.

'You're dead wrong, Marshal!' McLeod said in a taut voice. 'You've made a mistake – got the wrong Gann. Adam can't be no outlaw. He's stayed with us and helped us time after time, showing us the best road, leading us to the water places, saving our hides from Indians and outlaws and bandits like these here Mexicans. Man like that sure ain't no outlaw!'

A mutter of agreement followed Noah's words. Adam, stifling his pain, listened in silence, his hand closed about Sharon's.

'Ain't no mistake,' the lawman said flatly. 'Picture was plain.'

'What'd he do?' Jim Ritter demanded.

'Got in a scrap with some rancher, killed him. Judge gave him ten years in Yuma Prison. Was on his way there when he killed the U.S. marshal taking him and got away.'

'No, he didn't kill him!' McLeod said, his voice rising angrily. 'We was there – we seen it. Was the Indians that killed Slawson, if that was the name of the marshal.'

The lawman frowned. 'Name was Slawson, all right, but that don't help much. Still has to go to Yuma and serve–'

'No, I reckon not,' Jim Ritter drawled, and leveled the shotgun he was holding at the marshal. 'You or nobody else is going to take him to no prison.'

'My feelings, exactly,' Price declared, easing in beside Ritter, his weapon also pointing at the lawman.

McLeod nodded coldly. 'Reckon you see how it is, Marshal,' he said, his own rifle ready.

The lawman's features were stiff, angry. 'You'd best know what you're doing – it's a serious offense to obstruct the law–'

'What law?' Beth McLeod snapped. 'Where was the law when that bunch of outlaws took over our camp, tried to rob us? And where was it when these Mexicans drove us into here and would've killed us if it hadn't been for Adam?'

'I'm sorry, ma'am, but–'

'You bet you ain't got no answer to that!' McLeod said. 'It's men like Gann who make it possible for folks like us to stay alive in this country, and get where we're going, and we sure ain't letting no two-bit judge–'

'He shouldn't have been sentenced to prison for what he did,' Sharon said. 'It was a fair fight, and if that judge had been honest–'

'Just what I'd expect,' McLeod said, now leveling his gun also at the marshal. 'Best you mount up and ride on. You ain't taking Gann, not while we're able to pull a trigger!'

Adam shook his head. The situation was rapidly getting out of hand. He appreciated what the wagon train people were attempting to do for him, but he couldn't allow them to go through with it. Such would mean serious trouble for them – and the freedom he would gain would be no more than temporary.

'Never mind, Noah,' he said. 'I'm obliged to all of you, but I'd better go with him.'

A small cry escaped Sharon's throat, and jerked her hand free of his, she threw her arms about him, clung tightly.

'You're being smart,' the lawman said, and gestured to the several posse members over to one side watching narrowly. 'They're all sworn deputies. This thing could have come down to shooting, and some folks would've got hurt – maybe killed.'

'Likely,' Gann said, and pulling back from Sharon, took her chin in his hand and tipped her face up to his.

'It'll be all right. I'm giving you the name

of a friend of mine – a rancher up in the Wishbone Mountain country. I figure he'll go to the governor if I ask, and he's got enough pull to get me out, or at least get another trial before a fair judge. I'd like for you to write him–'

'I'll go see him,' Noah McLeod declared. 'And I'll talk to the governor myself! We'll get everybody we can working at it – means you, too, Marshal. You seen what he done for us here!'

The lawman said, 'Yeh, I did – and I've been thinking about that ten-year sentence for murder. Usually it calls for hanging. Must be something in what he says about it being a fair fight and a crooked judge. I'll do what I can for him. Now, I want to head back to Wickenburg before it gets too hot. Get that arm of yours doctored up, Gann, and say your good-byes so's we can start.'

Adam, his uninjured arm around Sharon, moved off toward the McLeod wagon. 'Way it sounds I maybe won't be gone too long.'

There were tears in her eyes as she looked up at him. 'We won't let it be long – we won't stop trying until you're free.'

His shoulders stirred. 'Something could backfire – best we think of that – and ten years is too long to ask you to wait–'

She raised a hand, placed her fingers against his lips, silencing his words. 'No matter – I'll still be waiting, Adam. You just be sure you come.'

He smiled. 'Just write me and tell me where you are, then set an extra place at the table. I'll be there,' he said, and bending over, kissed her firmly.

This Large Print Book, for people
who cannot read normal print,
is published under the auspices of

THE ULVERSCROFT FOUNDATION

... we hope you have enjoyed this book.
Please think for a moment about those
who have worse eyesight than you ...
and are unable to even read or enjoy
Large Print without great difficulty.

You can help them by sending a
donation, large or small, to:

**The Ulverscroft Foundation,
1, The Green, Bradgate Road,
Anstey, Leicestershire, LE7 7FU,
England.**
or request a copy of our brochure for
more details.

The Foundation will use all donations
to assist those people who are visually
impaired and need special attention
with medical research, diagnosis
and treatment.

Thank you very much for your help.